ALSO BY CANDACE FLEMING

FICTION

Ben Franklin's in My Bathroom!

The Fabled Fifth Graders of Aesop Elementary School

The Fabled Fourth Graders of Aesop Elementary School

NONFICTION

Amelia Lost: The Life and Disappearance of Amelia Earhart

The Great and Only Barnum: The Tremendous, Stupendous Life of Showman P. T. Barnum

STRONGHEART

WONDER DOG OF THE SILVER SCREEN

WRITTEN BY CANDACE FLEMING

ILLUSTRATED BY CALDECOTT MEDALIST ERIC ROHMANN

schwartz & wade books • new york

Text copyright © 2018 by Candace Fleming
Jacket art and interior illustrations copyright © 2018 by Eric Rohmann

All rights reserved. Published in the United States by Schwartz & Wade Books,
an imprint of Random House Children's Books,
a division of Penguin Random House LLC, New York.

Schwartz & Wade Books and the colophon are trademarks
of Penguin Random House LLC.

Visit us on the Web! rhcbooks.com

Educators and librarians, for a variety of teaching tools,
visit us at RHTeachersLibrarians.com

Library of Congress Cataloging-in-Publication Data
Names: Fleming, Candace, author. | Rohmann, Eric, illustrator.
Title: Strongheart : wonder dog of the silver screen / by Candace Fleming ; Illustrated by Eric Rohmann.
Description: First edition. | New York : Schwartz & Wade Books, [2018] | Summary: A German shepherd is transformed from Etzel, a police dog in Berlin, to Strongheart, a silent movie star that will need his best acting skills to prove himself innocent of attacking a girl.
Identifiers: LCCN 2017006773 (print) | LCCN 2017033654 (ebook) | ISBN 978-1-101-93412-8 (ebook) | ISBN 978-1-101-93410-4 (hardcover) | ISBN 978-1-101-93411-1 (library binding)
Subjects: LCSH: German shepherd dog—Juvenile fiction. | CYAC: German shepherd dog—Fiction. | Dogs—Fiction. | Working dogs—Fiction. | Motion pictures—Production and direction—Fiction.
Classification: LCC PZ10.3.F624 (ebook) | LCC PZ10.3.F624 St 2018 (print) | DDC [Fic]—dc23

The text of this book is set in 11.5-point font ParmaTypewriterPro.
The illustrations were rendered in oil paint.
Book design by Rachael Cole

Printed in the United States of America
1 3 5 7 9 10 8 6 4 2
First Edition

For Oxford—our very own Strongheart
—C.F. & E.R.

THE PUPPY

On a farm between the Bavarian Alps and the city of Berlin, a carefree puppy named Etzel played in a sun-washed barnyard.

He chased the chickens, barking in delight at their squawks and flaps.

He tipped over his water bowl, splashing and sliding in sloppy-fun mud.

And he gulped down the last of his kibble, licking the bowl to shiny emptiness.

At last, tired and full, he flopped onto the squirming puppies nestled in the curve of his mother's belly.

His sister, Greta, nipped his ear.

His brother, Otto, yipped a complaint.

But Etzel just wiggled down between them and sighed.

His family.

He had just closed his eyes, when—

"Here's a big, handsome one," a man's voice boomed.

Rough hands tore Etzel away from his family and held him high.

The puppy whimpered. His paws flailed in the suddenly cold air.

"Look at those markings," the voice boomed again. "Only purebred German shepherds have those. And what fine teeth . . ."

Rude fingers pulled back Etzel's lips.

"With the right training, they could tear a man to shreds. Should we take him?"

"*Ja*, take him," rumbled a second voice. "And we will turn him into the fiercest guard dog on the Berlin police force."

Etzel was shoved into a canvas bag.

His mother barked.

Greta and Otto yelped.

In the bag's darkness, Etzel whined.

ETZEL, ALL ALONE

The gate of the police kennel slammed shut behind Etzel.

For a moment, the puppy stood lost and shivering in the cement cell. Then he wobbled to the heavy door and, with a half-sobbing whine, *sniff-sniff*ed along its bottom.

Otto and Greta?

Mother?

He smelled nothing comforting. Nothing familiar.

Etzel fell back on his haunches. Opening his mouth, he let out a long, heartbroken wail.

"*Aaaaaaooooowwww!*"

The door banged open.

Etzel toddled forward, eager for pats and treats.

Instead, he was met with a sharp boot kick. "Silence!" shouted the man with the booming voice.

Etzel yelped and fell back.

But his punishment wasn't over.

Etzel curled tight into a trembling ball as the blows came. Again and again, until . . .

A new emotion—one the puppy had never before experienced—flashed through him. Whipping his head around, Etzel bared his tiny teeth.

"*That* is more like it," shouted the man. "Police dogs do not cry. They *fight*."

The man's words angered Etzel even more. A first, fierce growl rushed up his throat.

He sank his tiny teeth into tough boot leather.

"You think you are savage now, *mein Hund*? This is just the *start* of your training." The man gave his foot a rough shake, freeing his boot from Etzel's jaws.

The door slammed shut again.

Etzel crawled to his feet and limped into the darkest corner of his cell. Wary and alert, he lay with his head facing the door. He watched for the man to return.

Day turned to night, and the little dog grew cold and lonely. He missed his mother. He cried for her. He cried for Otto and Greta, too.

He cried too loud.

The man with the booming voice returned.

After that, Etzel no longer cried at night. But sometimes, when left alone in the fenced-in yard, he strayed off to a far corner. There he whimpered to himself . . . quietly.

HARD LESSONS

"Sit!" commanded the man with the booming voice.

Etzel furrowed his brow, as if trying to understand. It was his first day of police training, and he didn't know any of the commands. Not "come" or "walk" or "sit" or "stay."

"You will learn," said the man, slipping a thick chain collar with a leather leash attached to it around Etzel's neck. He led the dog around the windowless room.

Etzel had never walked on a leash before. He pulled and jerked every which way. Whirling, he nipped at the leather strap.

"Sit!" commanded the man again.

Etzel kept tugging.

Snap! The man yanked hard on the leash.

The collar tightened, squeezed, strangled.

Etzel gasped. Panicked and choking, he flailed at the end of the leash.

"Sit!" the man said again. He pushed the dog into a

sitting position, then eased the tension on the leash.

The collar released its vicious grip.

Etzel panted. Lowering his head, he looked at the cement floor.

"Walk!" came the next command.

But the puppy continued to hang his head.

"Walk!" The leash grew taut again. The collar squeezed and pinched.

Etzel's eyes opened wide. His body began to tremble.

Shouting the command one more time, the man dragged Etzel to his feet, forcing the puppy to stumble along on shaky legs. Around the room they went.

Walk, sit, *SNAP* went the leash.

Walk, sit, *SNAP* went the leash.

Again and again.

Day after day after day.

And just as the man had said, Etzel learned. He soon obeyed every command without question.

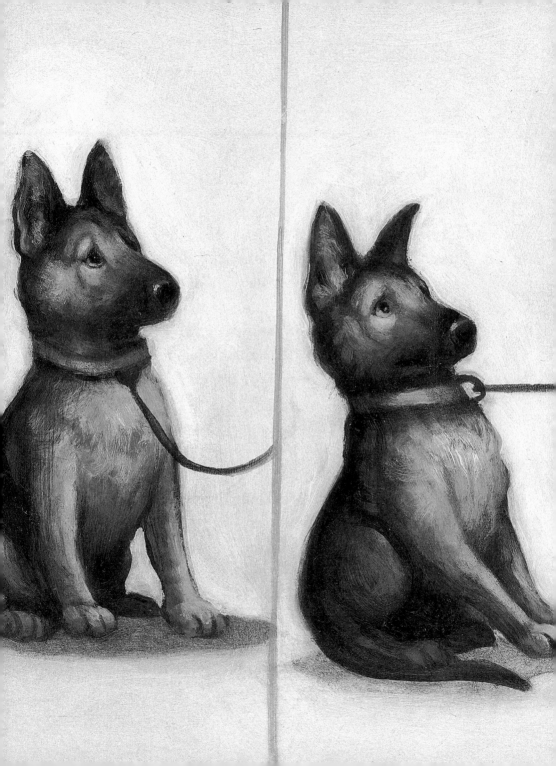

MORE HARD LESSONS

"Let's have some fun today, *ja?*" said the man. Opening the gate to the yard, he unhooked the puppy's leash and pushed him through.

Etzel stared. It had been nearly a month since his arrival at the police station. In that time, he had smelled and heard the other dogs. But he hadn't seen them. Not until now.

"Brrrr-woof!" He gamboled toward them, tail wagging.

A large dog with a fierce gaze named Teufel broke away from the pack. The hair along Teufel's spine stood on end. His lips curled back. Behind him, the other dogs stood tense and watchful.

Etzel dropped to his belly, hindquarters up, tail still wagging.

Teufel snarled.

Etzel sat back. He cocked his head, studying the other dog.

Teufel sprang. Darting in low, he slashed Etzel's shoulder with his fangs.

Etzel yelped and turned to lick his wound.

Teufel leaped in again. Knocking Etzel off his feet, he slashed the puppy's other shoulder before leaping clear.

The remaining dogs took this as a sign to attack. They rushed at Etzel, teeth bared.

Etzel scrambled back up to his feet. Tucking his tail, he ran as fast as he could.

The dogs pursued him, snapping at his heels. One sank his teeth into Etzel's hind leg.

Etzel stumbled and fell.

The snarling dogs circled.

Only the arrival of the man with the booming voice stopped the attack. With several savage kicks, he scattered the dogs. Teufel and the others slunk away, but not without a few last rumbles and growls.

Etzel lay on the ground, panting. His fur stood out in little tufts where the dogs' teeth had mauled him. Blood ran down his leg, and his shoulders burned.

From that day on, whenever he was left in the yard, he stalked around its edges. Keyed up and alert for attack, he met the dogs' snarls with terrible ones of his own. At the first sign of aggression, he didn't hesitate but rushed in, snapping and slashing.

"That one, he is a killer, *ja?*" said the man with the booming voice.

Soon, even Teufel kept his distance.

And so it was that by the end of his first year at the police station, Etzel was transformed.

Gone was the carefree puppy. In his place was a cold, uncaring police dog, who snapped at other dogs and trusted no one.

But sometimes, in the cold loneliness of his kennel, Etzel dreamed about the soft curve of his mother's belly and the playful nip of Greta's teeth on his ear. He dreamed about the smell of kibble on Otto's breath.

And in his sleep, Etzel would sigh.

A DOGGONE GOOD IDEA

Meanwhile, on the other side of the Atlantic, Americans had gone crazy for a new kind of entertainment: movies. In small towns and big cities all across the country, people flocked to their local movie theaters to be swept away by the stories flickering silently in black-and-white on the silver screen.

And they fell in love with the faces they saw up there—sweet Mary Pickford, bumbling Charlie Chaplin, mysterious and handsome Rudolph Valentino.

Audiences couldn't get enough of them.

Magazines couldn't stop photographing them.

Gossip reporters couldn't stop talking about their clothes and parties and romances.

They were stars—America's *first* movie stars.

In his bungalow office high in the Hollywood Hills, film director Larry Trimble slapped shut the latest issue of *Screenplay* magazine and turned to gaze out the window.

From his vantage, the Los Angeles valley spread out below him. It glowed with orange groves, palm trees, movie studios and . . .

"Possibilities," declared Larry.

Across the room, Jane Murfin sat at her typewriter, pounding out her latest screenplay.

Clickety-clack-ding! Clickety-clack-ding!

"Not again," she muttered to herself.

"Did you hear what I said, Jane? Possibilities."

"Hmmm," she said.

Clickety-clack-ding! Clickety-clack-ding!

"Can't you feel it? Now's the time. I tell you, the moviegoing public is holding its breath and waiting. Waiting, Jane, for something new and different. A fresh face on the big screen. Hollywood's next huge star."

Jane leaned forward. Crossing her arms over the typewriter, she arched one thin eyebrow. The corners of her red, Cupid's-bow lips quirked up. "Oh, sure . . . like who?"

Larry was silent.

Jane waited. She could always tell when he was noodling an idea. After making six films with him, she knew the signs: The loud sighs. The half-closed eyes. The way he ran his hand back and forth across his hair until it stood up in a brown halo. And when his idea was fully formed?

Larry snapped his fingers. "I've got it! Jane, what do you think of a *dog* movie star?"

Jane shrugged. "I think it sounds like a flat tire. After all, there are lots of dogs in the movies already."

"No, no, I'm not talking about a trick dog or some guy's pet. I'm talking about a real actor. Scripts written especially for him. Top billing."

"A lead actor that's a *dog*?" said Jane.

"Yeah, that's right."

"A movie-star dog?" Jane thought a moment. Larry had had crazier ideas. One time, he'd made a movie that showed nothing but the actors' hands and feet. Another time, he'd shot an entire film on his kitchen table with paper dolls. No wonder some people in Hollywood called him an oddball.

But not Jane. Never Jane. "A movie-star *dog*," she repeated.

"Not just any dog," said Larry. "A gorgeous dog. A noble dog. A smart, expressive, dramatic dog. A dog that can *act*."

Jane shook her head. "For Pete's sake, where are you going to find a dog like that?"

"I don't know, but he's out there . . . somewhere."

"No . . . no . . . no," grumbled Larry.

For the past two weeks, he'd been auditioning dogs—dozens and dozens of dogs. Among them, he'd screen-tested an Irish setter in Seattle. "Not noble enough," he grumbled.

He auditioned a husky in Houston. "Not handsome enough." And a bulldog in Buffalo. "You've got to be kidding!"

Desperate, he widened his search and boarded a ship bound for Europe. He crisscrossed England . . .

No star, he wired Jane.

France . . .

Still no star, he wired.

Italy . . .

Mamma mia! Where is our star? he wired yet again.

By the time he reached Germany, his confidence was lagging.

"Maybe this *was* a harebrained idea," he muttered to himself one morning. "Maybe no such dog exists."

Still, he trudged to a Berlin police station. He'd heard they were selling a few of their guard dogs.

The place did not look hopeful. It squatted on a street corner, gray and tomblike. Iron bars covered the windows. Barbed wire coiled across the top of brick walls. Surely he wouldn't find his star here. He turned away.

From inside the grim fortress came the muffled sound of barking.

Larry turned back. He shrugged. "Aw, what the heck? I'm here, aren't I?"

He pushed open the gate.

"Get out of the yard!" yelled a voice.

There came a bark like a clap of thunder, a crash, and a splinter of glass.

GRRRRRR!

Etzel leaped through the broken window and tore across the yard. Fur on end, teeth flashing, the dog sprang for Larry's throat.

"Stop!" Larry's voice sounded more pleading than commanding.

Etzel pulled back mid-lunge. Alert and suspicious, his muscles still tense, he stood unmoving.

So did Larry.

Dog and man stared at each other.

"Gorgeous," Larry whispered.

Etzel sniffed the air between them.

"Noble," added Larry. "But is he intelligent?" He pointed to the ground with a quivering finger, wordlessly commanding Etzel to sit.

Trained to obey, the dog sat back on his haunches. His eyes never left Larry's.

"Smart boy," the director praised. Feeling bolder, he reached for the dog.

"Careful!" the man with the booming voice warned from the other side of the fence. "That animal will tear your hand off before he'll let you pet him."

Larry's outstretched hand began to shake. Still, he stood his ground.

Etzel eyed the director's hand warily. He snarled.

Larry spoke gently, soothingly. "Be nice, now. Nice dog. *Gooood* dog."

Slowly, slowly, he lowered his hand toward the dog's head.

Etzel's ears flattened. He . . . SNAPPED!

But he didn't bite.

Larry managed to keep his hand steady. He kept crooning. "That's right. You don't really want to bite me, do you? You're a good boy. Good dog."

Etzel's snarl dwindled to a growl. The growl ebbed to a low rumble.

Larry's hand grazed Etzel's head.

Etzel shuddered and dropped his furious gaze. A sudden memory of his mother came to him: *she was turning her muzzle to him, lightly licking his neck.*

He looked up at Larry with sad, dark eyes.

Larry felt a tug at his heart.

"Dramatic," he whispered.

He had found his star.

HOMEWARD
BOUND

The taxi driver could not keep his eyes on the road. Again and again he glanced into his rearview mirror at the big dog crouched on the backseat. "Good doggie. Nice doggie," he muttered. His Adam's apple bobbed up and down nervously.

"Don't be afraid," soothed Larry.

"But he . . . he is a man-eater!" exclaimed the driver.

"I was talking to the dog," said Larry.

"Ack!" The driver glanced into the mirror again. Etzel's cold gaze met his. The dog licked his chops.

"Scheibenkleister!" yelped the driver. He mashed down the accelerator and sped for the docks.

Larry shrugged. "Not everyone appreciates star quality."

The pudgy passenger who huffed and puffed up the gangplank with her even pudgier schnauzer clasped tightly to her bosom didn't appreciate Etzel's star qualities, either.

And neither did the ship steward who burst into

Larry's stateroom with a dome-covered tray of food, and then—*"Yeooow!"*—burst right out again.

Etzel retreated to the far side of the room. Eyes narrowed and ears back, he watched his new owner suspiciously.

Larry watched Etzel, too. For a long time, the director didn't move or make a sound. When he finally spoke, his voice was soft. "Look at you, poor mutt. You're not really a tough guy, are you?"

The sound of Larry's voice caused the hair on Etzel's neck to rise. He growled.

Larry kept talking. "You just don't know how to be yourself, do you? Your noble character, your courage and sweetness are all there. I see them in you. But don't worry, boy. I'm going to help you find the real dog inside."

Etzel licked the growl from his lips.

Larry lifted the dome off the food tray and cut up the beefsteak he'd ordered. He held out a piece.

Etzel pricked his ears and sniffed suspiciously. At the same time, his body tensed, ready to spring away at the first sign of danger.

"Go ahead. It's okay. I know you're hungry."

Etzel didn't move.

Larry tossed the meat to him.

It landed between Etzel's front paws. The dog smelled it carefully. Then, eyes still locked on Larry, he took the piece in his mouth and swallowed.

"More?" asked Larry. He held out a second piece.

Again Etzel refused to take it.

Again Larry tossed it.

They did this over and over.

Finally, Larry picked up an especially thick and juicy piece. He held it out. This time he did not toss it.

Etzel licked his lips. Thrusting his head forward, ears flattened, he inched toward Larry's hand. And took the meat.

Nothing happened. No angry words. No boot kick.

Instead, another piece appeared.

And another.

And another, until the entire steak was gone.

Now Larry reached out with his empty hand. Slowly, he laid it on the dog's head. All the while he kept talking, letting Etzel get used to the sound of his voice. "I don't care if you keep growling and saying you hate me. I don't hate you back. I like you. You're a good boy."

Etzel made danger sounds deep in his throat. But he tolerated the hand patting his head, rubbing the base of his ears, stroking his back.

"See? That's not so bad, is it?" said Larry.

For a moment, the dog closed his eyes, and his head drooped, relaxed. But in the next, he stiffened and grew guarded. He remained that way . . .

Aloof.

Distant.

Wary.

All the way across the Atlantic Ocean.

A DOG NAMED STRONGHEART

Etzel's days soon became filled with the *clickety-clack-ding!, clickety-clack-ding!* of Jane's typewriter as she worked on a screenplay starring him. Time and again, she came to Larry's office door to study the dog.

"A coyote?" she would mutter. "Or a wolf?" Then she'd return to her typewriter.

Clickety-clack-ding!

Clickety-clack-ding!

One afternoon, Larry walked into Jane's office. "Listen, I've been thinking."

"Uh-huh."

"About Etzel."

"No kidding."

"Etzel," continued Larry. "What kind of name is *that* for a movie star? We need a different name, a new name, a name that will look good in lights."

"I'm way ahead of you, bub," said Jane. "How about . . ."

"Something tough yet tender," Larry cut in. "Something memorable and bold. Something like—"

"Will you quit flapping your gums and let me talk?" cried Jane.

"Ranger? No, no, too cowboy. Ace? Hmm . . . it doesn't suit him. What about Lightning? Blaze? Maybe—"

"Strongheart," blurted Jane.

Larry blinked. "Strongheart," he repeated. "Say, that's pretty good. Strongheart!" Larry turned to the dog. "What do you think, boy?"

Etzel, now Strongheart, didn't move a muscle.

"Strongheart," Larry said again.

The dog stared straight ahead.

"*That's* a problem," said Jane. "Etzel . . . Strongheart . . . it doesn't matter what you call him. Not once has he ever wagged his tail, or barked just for the heck of it. Has he ever nuzzled your hand or begged for treats?" She didn't give Larry a chance to answer. "Nope, he waits for a command before eating, sleeping, sitting . . . anything!"

Larry rested his hand on Strongheart's head. He tried to imagine what it felt like to be so controlled and in check all the time, to bottle up your feelings and suppress your instincts. It would be like jail, he thought. Like living in jail.

Jane came around from behind her desk. She lowered herself to look the dog in the eye. "Do you think we made a mistake? Do you think he's the wrong dog?"

"He's the right dog," said Larry. "He has so much love and loyalty to give. I know it. I just haven't figured out how to reach him yet."

He rubbed behind the dog's ears.

Strongheart tolerated it.

"Poor pooch," said Jane. "He's so serious. Do you think he's ever played, even as a puppy?"

"Play?" Larry repeated. He snapped his fingers. "That's it! Jane, you're a genius."

TEACHING A DOG
A NEW TRICK

Larry led Strongheart into the backyard after breakfast the next morning. Pulling out a red rubber ball,
he squeezed it invitingly.

SQUEAK! went the ball.

"Looks fun, huh?" said Larry.

Strongheart cocked his head.

Larry put the ball on the ground right in front of the dog. "Can you fetch?"

Strongheart picked up the ball. Stiffly and precisely, he placed it in Larry's outstretched hand.

"Good boy!" he exclaimed.

Strongheart gave him a serious look.

"Let's do it again, okay?"

Larry put down the ball.

Strongheart picked it up.

Over and over.

Again and again.

Then Larry said, "Let's try something a little harder." He placed the ball halfway across the yard. "Can you fetch that?"

Strongheart immediately marched over to the ball, picked it up, and brought it back.

"Splendid, buddy! You're magnificent! Good boy!" Larry patted the dog's head.

Strongheart's ears perked up.

Just like before, they did this again and again.

Next, Larry placed the ball on the far side of the yard.

"You know what I want you to do."

Strongheart did. Trotting over, he scooped up the ball. He dropped it into Larry's open hand.

"Buddy boy, you're a natural!" praised Larry. He thumped the dog's sides.

The tip of Strongheart's tail wiggled.

"Ready for something tougher?" Larry asked. He raised the ball above his head and gave it a *SQUEAK!*

Strongheart licked his lips.

And Larry flung the ball. It bounced playfully across the yard. "Go on, buddy, fetch!"

But Strongheart just stared after it.

"You can do it," encouraged Larry.

The dog stood there, uncertain.

"I understand. Learning new things isn't easy. But you can do this." He retrieved the ball. "Ready?" He bounced it again. "Fetch!"

Finally, Strongheart obeyed. Scrambling after the ball, he picked it up and brought it back.

Over and over it went. Bounce, chase, praise, then Larry throwing the ball again, each time a little wilder.

It bounced over the dog's head, and Strongheart had to jump for it.

It bounced off the fence, and Strongheart had to dart after it.

It ricocheted off a lawn chair and ... *SMACK!* ... struck the dog on his nose before rolling deep beneath a holly bush.

Strongheart froze. He suddenly looked awkward and self-conscious. Not since his early days of training had he made such a mess of a command. He bowed his head as if expecting punishment.

"It's okay, buddy. We're just having fun. Get the ball."

Strongheart swung his big head back and forth between Larry and the bush.

Larry could tell the dog was wavering. Should he behave like a serious police dog? Or should he abandon his training and dive after the ball? "Please, boy," he begged. "Play with me."

At that moment, a memory came to Strongheart: *he was splashing through barnyard puddles, chasing squawking chickens, rolling and tumbling with Greta and Otto.*

The dog whined, letting out long, reedy notes.

"What's the matter?" Larry took a step toward him.

Strongheart lowered his head and barked. At first it was weak, almost the squeak of a puppy. But with each woof he grew louder ... and louder ... and louder ... until he lifted his head and howled.

"Aaaaawoooo!"

He pulled back his lips as if he was laughing.

Larry threw his head back and laughed, too.

Then Strongheart bounded over to the bush, dove beneath it, and grabbed the ball. But he didn't return it to Larry's outstretched hand. Instead, he raced around the yard with it, his head and tail held high.

Larry ran after him. "Give me that ball, you naughty animal," he teased.

Strongheart played tag.

Larry lunged for the dog.

Strongheart played keep-away.

Then Larry tried to grab the ball out of the dog's mouth.

Strongheart played tug-of-war.

All the noise drew Jane away from her typewriter. "Well, I'll be zozzled," she said, watching as they chased each other around the yard.

At long last, Larry fell back into the sweet grass, panting and laughing.

And Strongheart dropped down beside him.

He gave his red rubber ball a loud and joyful . . .
SQUEAK!

STRONGHEART REVEALS HIS SECRETS

With each passing day, Strongheart grew more trusting. As he did, his talents and graces—trapped for so long inside him—began to reveal themselves.

Gentleness.

Generosity.

A sense of humor.

Then one night, the dog bumped open Larry's bedroom door.

Larry turned and his eyes widened. Since arriving in Hollywood, Strongheart had insisted on sleeping alone on the living room's hard tile floor. He refused blankets. He turned up his nose at pillows. But now here he stood, staring at the pajama-clad director.

Larry patted the bed. "Do you want to sleep with me?"

Strongheart jumped up.

"I guess that's a yes," said Larry. He rolled to the far side, making room for the dog.

Strongheart snuffled the blankets. Then he began spinning in a small circle, as if tamping down a patch of invisible grass.

Around and around.

Around and around.

Around and . . .

"All right, already," grumbled Larry.

Strongheart flopped down and let out a loud sigh.

And Larry rolled over and switched off the light.

The two lay side by side in the dark.

Slowly, Larry reached out and laid his hand on the dog's neck. Beneath his fingers, the fur was thick and springy and impossibly soft. "Good boy," he whispered.

Strongheart inched closer. He dabbed Larry's arm with his tongue.

"First kiss," murmured Larry before drifting off to sleep.

Hours later, Larry awoke to find Strongheart's back end smashed against his face.

"Hey, come on. Turn it the other way," complained Larry. He gave the dog a shove.

Sleepily, reluctantly, Strongheart obeyed.

But minutes later . . .

"Knock it off, Strongheart!" cried Larry. "Either lay your head in the right direction or get off the bed."

With an exasperated sigh, the dog once again righted himself.

But not for long.

"That's it!" Larry shouted. "Off the bed."

Strongheart jumped to the floor and watched Larry with unblinking eyes.

Perhaps it was the late hour, or the way the shadows fell across the dog's face, but Strongheart looked as if he knew everything that was being said to him. *Really* knew. Not in the owner-dog command sort of way, but on a deeper level. Larry ventured, "Do you . . . understand me?"

In response, the dog's tail swished back and forth across the floor.

"You get what's on my mind," clarified Larry. "You grasp my point of view. You . . . you . . . comprehend my thoughts and feelings."

This time Strongheart thumped his tail . . . *hard.*

Larry ran a hand over his face. "I'm so tired, I'm delusional," he muttered to himself.

But to the dog, he said, "Listen, if you and I are going to go on sleeping together, we're going to have to establish some rules. I'm willing to give you half the bed. I can even put up with your infernal circling. But this sleeping with your rear end in my face is *out*!"

At this, Strongheart grabbed Larry's pajama sleeve in his teeth and tugged him toward the bedroom window. Then, releasing the sleeve, he grabbed one of the curtains in his mouth. He held on to it a moment before letting it drop back. *"Woof!"* He looked from the window to the bed.

Larry understood as clearly as if Strongheart were speaking English. The former police dog wanted to sleep facing the window. If a burglar tried to get in that way, Strongheart wouldn't have to waste time turning around before leaping into action.

"Why didn't you say so earlier?"

Huffing and puffing, Larry turned the bed around. Then—after Strongheart spun a few more circles—man and dog flopped onto the pillows. Both their heads pointed toward the window.

Strongheart quickly fell asleep.

But Larry lay awake, his thoughts whirling. He'd uncovered two secrets about his dog that night.

First and most mind-boggling, Strongheart had understood—*truly* understood. And in his dog wisdom, he'd made it possible for Larry to understand him, too.

And second?

The director shoved the shepherd's head off his shoulder.

Strongheart was a drooler.

THE SILENT CALL

Clickety-clack-ding!
Clickety-clack-ding!
Clickety-clack...

"Done!" declared Jane. With a flourish, she pulled the paper from her typewriter. Adding it to the pile on her desk, she carried it out to the backyard, where Larry and Strongheart lounged in the shade of the jacaranda tree.

She waved the pages in the air. "Guess what I've got!" she sang out.

"You've finished the screenplay!" cried Larry.

"It's not the telephone book," joked Jane.

Larry rubbed his hands together. "Well, let's hear it."

Jane pulled up a lawn chair.

And Strongheart scooped up his red rubber ball. *SQUEAK! SQUEAK! SQUEAK!*

"Put that down and listen," said Larry.

The dog let the toy roll out of his mouth. Ears straight, head cocked, he gave Jane his undivided attention.

Jane shook her head in wonder. "That dog constantly amazes me." Then she turned to the first page of the script. *"The Silent Call,"* she read.

"Terrific title!" said Larry. "I can already see it on theater marquees. Can't you, boy?"

Strongheart gave the script an appreciative lick. Then he sat back on his haunches and waited for more.

"The film's main character is Flash, an animal that is half dog, half wolf." She turned to Strongheart. "That's your part."

The dog thumped his tail.

"When the film opens," Jane continued, "Flash is working on a ranch, guarding livestock. But while his master is away, he is falsely accused of killing sheep. Sentenced to death by the local ranchers, Flash escapes into the mountains, where he faces hunger, freezing temperatures, and snarling wolves."

Larry whooped. "Thrills, chills, and adventure!"

"Eventually, Flash finds happiness with a beautiful she-wolf."

"Romance!" exclaimed Larry.

"He and his mate have puppies."

"Heartwarming family moments!"

"But when the real sheep killer kidnaps his master's wife, Flash must leave his own family to save her."

"Drama and suspense!" Larry scrambled to his feet.

"That script hits on all sixes. I've said it before, and I'll say it again. Jane, you're a genius." Grabbing her by the waist, he whirled her around.

Strongheart joined in, bouncing, swirling, barking. He leaped up to—*SLURRRP!*—the screenwriter's face and then—*SLURRRP!*—the director's.

"What's come over you two!" squealed Jane. "Larry, put me down. Ohhh!"

Larry gave her one last mighty twirl.

"Wheeeee!"

"Brrr-woof!"

Ker-bump!

The three landed in a heap on the grass.

The impact knocked some ideas loose.

Larry snapped his fingers. "We'll film on location in the Sierra Nevada Mountains," he declared. "Real snow. Real caves. Real cliffs."

"And a real dog," said Jane.

"A real *good* dog," added Larry.

ON LOCATION

The crew on location bustled. Carpenters built log cabins from plywood and canvas. Property men rushed about carrying props, costumes, and clapboards. Above it all, on a specially made platform, Pete the cameraman grunted as he attached his bulky hand-cranked camera to a big tripod.

All the activity made Strongheart's fur bristle.

"Easy, boy." Larry laid a hand on the dog's neck. "You know I'll never ask you to do anything that isn't right, and I'll always protect you."

Strongheart—ball in mouth—looked at him warily.

"I promise," added Larry.

Strongheart lowered his hackles.

"Hey, fellas, over here!" hollered Jane. Holding back the flap of the makeup tent, she waved.

Inside, lighted mirrors glowed golden through the haze of fine white face powder. The waxy smell of greasepaint hung heavy in the air.

Strongheart sneezed.

A gaggle of women wearing identical pink smocks turned. One of them, her gray hair pulled so tightly into a bun that her eyes squinted, *clap-clap*ped her hands. "Ladies, to work!" she commanded.

Like a swarm of pink insects, they swooped down on Strongheart.

He dropped his ball and bared his teeth.

They ignored him.

"Agnes, apply more mud to the left hind leg," the woman instructed. "Tease that fur into tangles and mats, Louise. And don't forget the burrs. You hear me, Bonita? I want lots and lots of burrs. This dog must look wretched and draggled, as if he has wandered lost and forlorn in the wilderness for days."

Snip-snip!

Poof-poof!

Spritz-spritz!

"*Wurrr!*" grumbled Strongheart.

"Don't forget my promise," Larry reminded him.

At the other end of the tent, actor Ed Brady snickered. "That's our *star*? What's he going to do in the big fight scene? Attack me with his scary red ball?"

This time it was Larry's turn to bristle.

"It looks to me like this is just another one of your oddball ideas, Trimble," said Ed, standing up.

Jane placed a calming hand over Larry's clenched fist. "Actually," she said to the actor, "Strongheart is very convincing as an attack dog."

"I'd like to see that," snorted Ed.

"He asked for it."

"Larry . . . ," Jane cautioned.

The director pointed at Ed. "Get the bad guy, Strongheart!"

Suddenly all teeth and on-end fur, he leaped at Ed.

"Whoa . . . whoa . . . whoa!" yelled the actor. He ducked and covered his face with his arms.

Strongheart plowed into him. Snarling, knocking Ed about, he tore the sleeve of the actor's cowboy costume to shreds.

"Call him off! Call him off!"

"Down," said Larry.

Strongheart dropped to the floor.

Ed pointed a trembling finger at the dog. "That . . . that . . . *beast* has no business on this set. He's a . . . a . . . killer!"

"Applesauce," scoffed Jane. "He was just acting." She picked up Strongheart's ball and tossed it to him.

SQUEAK!

"Acting? He tried to eat me!"

"Do you have a single scratch or tooth mark anywhere on your body?" asked Larry.

Ed patted his arms and legs. "Not a one," he said incredulously.

"You see?" said Larry. "Strongheart was merely *playing* the part of a ferocious dog."

"Convincing, wasn't he?" added Jane.

"And without any acting lessons." Larry thumped the dog's side. "Strongheart is a natural."

"He sure is!" declared the woman with the bun. She crawled out from under the table where she'd taken cover.

"Now shake and be friends," said Larry. "We've got a film to make."

Strongheart held out a paw.

And Ed weakly shook it.

Then the dog set off to meet the rest of the cast and crew.

"Put her there, champ!" said the man playing the rancher.

"Nice to meet you, Mr. Strongheart," said the woman playing the rancher's wife.

Strongheart tolerated the wardrobe worker's cooing and cuddling.

"Ooooh, what a big, gorgeous brute you are!"

He even accepted a corner of Pete the cameraman's pimiento cheese and horseradish sandwich.

"It's my own recipe. Delish, huh?"

The dog forced it down.

Then Larry hollered through his megaphone. "Places!"

Crew members scrambled into position.

And Strongheart found himself in front of the camera.

ACTION!

Larry bent down and looked the dog in the eye. "This is it, boy. Your first scene. Are you nervous?"

Strongheart touched his nose to the director's.

"You shouldn't be. Remember, films don't have dialogue or musical scores like theater performances. They're silent. That means the story is told through action, expression, and gesture. And if anybody is a natural at portraying emotions, it's you. Got it?"

"Woof!"

"Great. So here's your direction." Larry's voice took on the mood of the scene. "You've been banished to the wilderness, a cold, lonely place without human companionship. And yet, you feel strangely at home here. You feel drawn to the mountains. Your wolf instincts are calling to you. Understand?"

"Hold on," interjected Pete. "Aren't you going to call out commands? Bribe him with treats?"

Larry shook his head. "Strongheart will be *acting,* not doing circus tricks."

"Oh, brother," said Pete. Rolling his eyes, he took his place behind the camera.

Larry took his seat in the director's chair. Lifting his

megaphone to his lips once more, he shouted, "Action!"

Strongheart sat.

Thik-thik-thik-thik went the camera as Pete cranked its handle.

"Come on, dog. Show us what you've got," urged Ed, who stood and watched with the other actors.

But Strongheart didn't move a muscle.

A minute passed.

"Now might be the time to pull out those treats," suggested Pete.

Thik-thik-thik-thik.

"Maybe a command or two?"

Larry held up his hand. "Give him another minute."

Thik-thik-thik-thik.

At last, the dog seemed to make up his mind. Getting to his feet, he shook himself, turned around, and strode off.

Around a stand of fir trees.

Along a rocky trail.

Up . . . up . . . up to the very edge of a high mountain cliff.

Pete swiveled the camera, keeping the dog in the frame.

Jane gasped. "What's he doing?"

"I think he's acting," said Larry.

Posed with the snow-capped mountain towering above him and the silence of the wilderness surrounding him, the dog gazed down on the valley. He looked gorgeous. Noble. Dramatic.

Pete whistled through his teeth. "I don't believe it."

But Strongheart wasn't done yet. Lifting his head, he sniffed the icy air and . . . *"Ah-woooo!"*

It was the perfect theatrical touch.

"That dog is the cat's whiskers!" exclaimed Jane.

"That dog is a star," added Larry.

Strongheart whipped his head around to face them. A savage look came into his eyes, and the hair around his neck went straight up. Without waiting for Larry to shout "Cut," the dog charged off the rocky ledge and made for the crew.

People screamed and scattered.

But Strongheart only had eyes for the pudgy, balding studio hand standing beside Jane.

The man turned and started running.

Strongheart lunged. Catching him by one of his ankles, he threw the man flat on his back.

"Stop! Stop!" commanded Larry.

Strongheart didn't obey. Seizing the front of the man's jacket in his fangs, he shook with furious might. Out flew a gold bracelet, several wallets, and a silver fountain pen.

"Hey, that's mine!" cried Jane. She picked up the pen.

"My bracelet!" exclaimed the wardrobe worker.

"Thief!" shouted Pete.

"Grrrrr," rumbled Strongheart. Teeth bared, he stood on the man's chest until the security guards came.

"How did he know?" asked Jane when calm settled back over the set.

"Once a police dog, always a police dog, I guess," said Larry.

Strongheart shook himself, gave the back of Jane's hand a dab of his tongue, and flopped at her feet.

Ed Brady plucked his wallet off the ground and slipped it back into his pocket. Turning to the dog, he stuck out his hand. "I owe you a shake of gratitude!"

"And oooh, oooh, I'm going to give you the biggest hug ever," squealed the wardrobe worker.

"And *I'm* going to reward you with the rest of my sandwich," added Pete. He unwrapped his leftovers.

Strongheart tolerated their gratitude.

THE BIG SCENE

The days rushed by in a flurry of cranking camera and snapping clapboards. As star of the film, Strongheart appeared in almost every scene.

Escape scenes.

Chase scenes.

Fight scenes.

In every one, he thrilled.

The film's last scene took place at the mouth of a cave. In earlier shots, the cave had been the dog's happy home, where he lived with his wolf wife and their three pups—all played by stuffed toy animals. Now, however, property men had blocked the cave's entrance with papier-mâché boulders. They'd filled the surrounding area with piles of rubble and debris.

Larry laid his hand on the dog's head. "This is it, buddy—*the big scene.*"

"Will you stop calling it that?" said Jane. "You'll make him nervous."

"But it *is* the big scene," replied Larry. "It's the story's emotional climax. It's the heart. All the other scenes have been working up to this moment. Everything hinges on it."

"Applesauce!" exclaimed Jane. She knelt down and rubbed the dog's ears. "Don't listen to him, Strong-heart. Just do your best."

"May I remind you that *I'm* the director?" said Larry.

"Who's directing?" replied Jane, winking at Strong-heart.

It was Larry's turn to kneel in front of the dog. "Remember, buddy, this is when you learn that an explosion has trapped your family inside the cave."

Strongheart cocked his head.

"It's a heart-wrenching scene. A real tearjerker."

Strongheart's ears stood up straight.

"I need you to bring everything you've got. Can you do that for me, boy?"

Strongheart licked Larry's nose.

"Then let's shoot it."

Larry took his place in his chair. He knew Strongheart was good. But this scene? Even Hollywood's
greatest actors would find it a challenge. He wiped a
sweaty palm down the front of his jacket. Then, raising
the megaphone to his dry lips, he croaked, "Action!"

Thik-thik-thik-thik.

Strongheart trotted into the scene, tail wagging,
with a toy duck in his mouth.

"That's right, boy," directed Larry. "You're happy.
You're bringing a delicious dinner to your family.
You don't know what's happened yet. That's right. . . .
Move closer. . . . You see the tragedy now. . . . You can't
believe it."

Strongheart let the duck drop from his mouth. He took a stumbling step forward. Stopped. He took another step forward. Stopped.

"There's no way to save them," Larry went on. "You've lost everything that matters to you . . . everything in the world."

Strongheart turned his head and gazed into the distance. He seemed to be looking into the years ahead without his family.

Thik-thik-thik-thik.

"That's it," said Larry. "That's terrific, boy. *Hold it. . . .*"

A memory came to Strongheart: *Rough hands were ripping him from his family. Stuffing him into a bag.*

Strongheart fell to the ground. Howling, he covered his face with his paw.

"That's impossible!" cried Ed Brady.

"Dogs can't do that!" exclaimed Pete.

"Holy mackerel!" Jane gasped. "He looks like he's *crying.*"

For several long moments, the dog lay there, sides heaving. Finally, he lifted his head and looked deep into the camera with an anguished expression. Then he dropped his head back to his forepaws. Life, his actions seemed to say, had no meaning for him anymore.

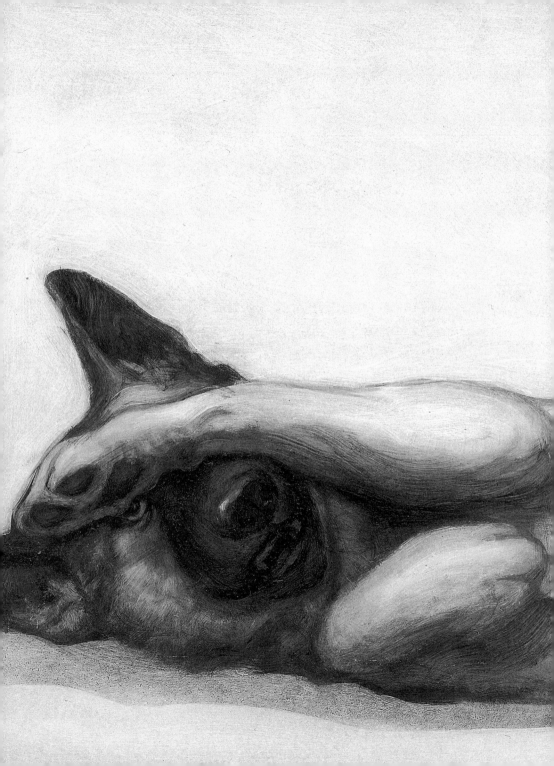

Silence—broken only by the camera's grinding and the crew's sniffling—fell over the set.

Thik-thik-thik-thik.

At last, Larry pulled out his handkerchief. "Wow, Strongheart. Wow, buddy." He wiped his eyes and blew his nose. "Cut. Print. That's a wrap."

FAME!

Larry fumbled with the radio dial.

Sizzling, scratching static filled the bungalow.

"Come on, come on," he muttered, making adjustments.

More static.

"Blasted thing."

Then—

"Hello from Hollywood, that fabulous city filled with stars, studios, and . . . *gossip*!"

"She's on!" called Larry.

Strongheart bounded into the living room. Jumping up onto the couch, he squeezed between Larry and Jane.

All three leaned forward to listen to the nasally voice of gossip reporter Lulu Popper.

Lulu was the most influential woman in Hollywood. With her glib, sharp tongue, she could make or break a movie . . . *and* its star. What would she say about Strongheart in *The Silent Call*?

"This better be good," said Larry.

"Today's tittle-tattle concerns a Tinsel Town new-comer," clucked Lulu. "Who, you ask? Why, Strong-heart, of course! Discovered by oddball director Larry Trimble, the four-legged actor has all the makings of a star."

"Did you hear that?" squealed Jane. "She used the word *star*!"

"She used the word *oddball*," grumbled Larry.

Strongheart nuzzled his big head against Larry's arm sympathetically.

Lulu went on. "Just last night, I attended an advance screening of Strongheart's first-ever movie, *The Silent Call*. Listeners, he is a marvel. His rakish good looks rival Valentino's. And his acting ability is—dare I say it—more human than a human's. I confess, I am absolutely *maaaad* for the dog."

"Egads! She likes it!" whopped Larry.

"Shhhh!" said Jane.

"The film opens tomorrow in theaters from Oregon to Maine," continued Lulu. "You *must* see it. Once you have, I know you'll agree: Strongheart is the brightest new star in Hollywood's already-glittering heaven. And remember, dear listeners, you heard it *here* first."

Larry switched off the radio. For once, he was speechless.

But Jane wasn't. "Darb!" she exclaimed. "Our dog's going to be famous."

Across the country that week, wherever *The Silent Call* played, people stood in line for blocks waiting to buy tickets. In the theater, they settled expectantly into their seats. Then the house lights dimmed. The velvet curtains parted. The music from the orchestra swelled dramatically.

Audiences had never seen a leading actor like this one. Strongheart somersaulted off cliffs and leaped over mountain gorges. His facial expressions were by turns tragic and tender, fierce and sorrowful. And in the flickering darkness of hundreds of theaters, moviegoers gasped . . . cheered . . . sobbed.

When the houselights came back up, audiences blinked. There was a moment's silence—a drawn-out pause—as transported moviegoers returned to reality. Then they leaped to their feet, clapping and whistling.

"Bravo!" they shouted. "Hooray for Strongheart!"

By week's end, *The Silent Call* was America's number one movie.

And Strongheart was its number one star.

At Larry's bungalow, the telephone jangled morning and night as requests, offers, and invitations poured in.

Hordes of reporters begged for stories about the star.

"Does Strongheart snack on steak from a silver bowl?" they asked. "Does he wear a diamond collar?"

Swarms of photographers snapped the star's picture. They posed the dog on mountain cliffs and sandy beaches, beside starlets and celebrities. He was photographed pretending to operate a movie camera and driving a Ford Model T Roadster. The cover of *Screen Digest* showed him playing golf. *Photoplay*'s cover had him ordering steak at a fancy restaurant. And *Hollywood Today*?

"We've come up with a marvelous idea," gushed the magazine's editor the morning of their photo shoot. "We want Strongheart to sit in Mr. Trimble's director's chair wearing . . . Are you ready? A beret." She clapped with excitement. "Isn't that ingenious?"

Strongheart backed away and looked at Larry hard, as if he were trying to say something.

"What?" Larry asked.

Strongheart stared at him.

"You think the beret is stupid?"

Strongheart twitched his ears and raised his eyebrows.

"You refuse to wear it?"

Strongheart flopped down.

"I'll tell her," said Larry.

When *Hollywood Today* hit newsstands the following week, Strongheart's noble profile gazed moodily from the cover. No beret. No director's chair.

"That's a swell picture," declared Jane when she saw it. She kissed Strongheart's nose. "You are one gorgeous fellow, you know that?"

"Brrr-woof!" he barked.

"Modest, too," added Larry.

The phone rang yet again.

"This is R. J. Penrose, president of the National Dog Food Company," said the voice on the other end. "We would very much like to rename our product after your dog. That is, of course, if Strongheart will endorse it."

Larry covered the receiver. "What do you think?" he whispered to the dog.

Strongheart *smack-smack-smack*ed his chops, as if he had peanut butter stuck to the roof of his mouth.

"I'll ask," said Larry. He spoke into the receiver. "How do we know your dog food tastes good?"

"Why, I'll prove it," declared Mr. Penrose.

That afternoon the doorbell rang.

It was the company president himself, and he was holding a can of National Dog Food.

As Larry and Strongheart watched, Mr. Penrose dug a spoon deep into the chopped meat and lifted it to his mouth. A dollop of brown gravy dripped onto one of his wing tips.

Strongheart helpfully licked it away.

Mr. Penrose chewed and swallowed. "Mmmm, delicious." He went back for a second mouthful.

Strongheart wiggled forward and stood up on his hind legs. Face to face with the president, he opened his mouth.

"You want a little tasteroo, too?" said Mr. Penrose. He popped a bite into the dog's mouth.

Strongheart rolled the dog food around in his mouth before swallowing. He waggled his ears as if he was trying to decide whether he liked it.

"Woof," he decided.

Mr. Penrose clapped Larry on the back. "Didn't I tell you?"

Sitting shoulder to shoulder on the front stoop, dog and company president finished the can.

FINAL

Los Angeles Chronicle

German Shepherd Becomes Most Popular Breed in America

Weeks later, Strongheart Dog Food appeared in grocery stores from coast to coast. Every can featured a picture of the movie star dog. *My favorite dog food,* read the back label. *Faithfully, Strongheart.*

But it wasn't until breakfast one morning that Larry fully realized the heights of his dog's fame. He was buttering toast for Strongheart and reading the *Los Angeles Chronicle* when he suddenly whistled. "Will you look at that!"

He held out the newspaper so Strongheart could see.

GERMAN SHEPHERD BECOMES MOST POPULAR BREED IN AMERICA, read the headline.

"Everybody wants a Strongheart," said Larry. He ruffled the dog's ears. "They're going to be disappointed, though. You're one of a kind."

Strongheart laid his head in Larry's lap. His tail *thump-thump*ed on the kitchen floor.

The director understood completely. Strongheart thought Larry was one of a kind, too.

PUBLICITY STUNT

Clickety-clack-ding!
Clickety-clack-ding!
Jane was writing a new screenplay for Strongheart.

"I'm calling it *The Love Master*," she said. "And it's the bee's knees, if I do say so myself."

"Let's hear it," said Larry.

Strongheart sat up. He wiggled his ears this way and that, trying to catch all the words.

"The story centers around a dog-sled race," explained Jane.

"Strongheart's character endures days of toil—pulling, always pulling—over snow-covered mountains and glistening glaciers. He grows exhausted. So he goes off in search of help, and finds another dog—a female dog."

At the word *dog,* Strongheart bolted to his feet. A memory came to him: *Teufel slashing and attacking; the other dogs chasing and circling.* Planting himself in front of Larry, he stared. He didn't wag his tail. He didn't move a muscle. He just stared as if he had something important to tell him.

Larry nudged the dog aside. "What breed is this female dog?" he asked Jane.

Jane shrugged. "I hadn't thought. It could be any breed, I suppose."

Strongheart whined. He smacked Larry's leg with a heavy paw.

Ignoring him, Larry snapped his fingers. "Maybe this is a harebrained idea, but what if we asked moviegoers to help find our leading lady?"

"That's a swell plan!" exclaimed Jane. "We could launch a nationwide search."

"Place full-page ads in newspapers and magazines," added Larry.

"And on the appointed day, hold open auditions at the studio!" cried Jane.

"*Wurrr! Woof-woof-woof!*"

Both Larry *and* Jane ignored him.

"This idea is the berries!" whooped Jane. "The whole country will be buzzing about Strongheart's next film."

"Before one frame is even shot," hooted Larry.

Strongheart stalked to the door. Turning, he growled, making his feelings on the subject clear. He did not like other dogs. He did not trust them.

Neither Larry nor Jane was listening.

Looking insulted and still making danger sounds in his throat, the dog clamped the knob in his jaws and turned. The door swung open.

Behind him, he heard Jane ask, "What if the female can't act?"

"Who cares? Our boy is actor enough for *two* dogs."

Strongheart marched into the backyard.

"*Wurrrr!*"

DOGS!

On the day of the audition, the studio lot swarmed with dogs.

Panting.

Snapping.

Wrestling.

Napping.

And waiting for their shot at stardom.

One by one, Jane beckoned them
onto the stage and into the bright
circle of the arc light.

Each dog was asked to trot left . . . trot right . . . face the camera, and bark.

Strongheart dropped his head to his paws. He lay there in miserable silence as a line of would-be leading ladies passed before him.

Pedigrees. Hounds. Mutts.

Now and again, he rumbled.

So did Larry, but for a completely different reason.

"Two hundred and fifty-six dogs," he groused as the sun began to dip behind the Hollywoodland sign. "And not one is right for the part."

"How many are left?" asked Jane.

Larry glanced at his clipboard. "Three. Just three."

Jane frowned. "I'll have to rewrite the script. Cut the female role."

At her words, Strongheart scrambled to all fours. Bouncing and swirling and tossing around barks, he made it clear that Jane should begin rewriting at once.

Larry called out, "Next!"

A Saint Bernard stepped onto the stage.

The director shook his head. "Too big. Next!"

A Pekingese took her place.

"Too little. Next!"

Strongheart dove beneath the director's chair to retrieve his rubber ball. It was time to go home . . . and *without* a leading lady. His tail wagged wildly. He gave the ball a loud and happy *SQUEAK!*

"Burrr-arrrf!" he heard.

It was a pleasant bark, soft and musical.

Strongheart backed out from under the chair and looked.

Onstage, in the halo of light, stood a slim silver-coated German shepherd.

She stared at Strongheart with pale blue eyes.

He glared back.

"Burrr-arrrf," she barked again. Her fluffy tail wagged alluringly.

Strongheart let his ball drop to the floor. *PLOP.* It was obvious he knew what Larry would say next.

"That's her! That's our leading lady."

THE LOVE MASTER

Filming began two weeks later on the studio lot on shooting stage number 21. Property men had transformed the cavernous building into the wintry north. Fake snow. Fake mountains. Fake pines.

"Pretty swell, huh?" enthused Jane the first day.

But Strongheart wasn't admiring the scenery. All his attention was focused on the slender German shepherd sashaying toward them. He blinked. The creature's toenails were painted pink. She had on a leopard-skin coat. She smelled—he flared his nostrils—like gardenias. He curled his lips.

"None of that," said Larry.

Strongheart licked away his snarl.

"And here is Lady Jule," trilled her owner, Mrs. Vanderbeek.

"Hello, Jule girl." Larry reached out to ruffle her ears.

"Oh, dear me, stop!" gasped Mrs. Vanderbeek. "You mustn't pet her unless *she* has invited you to do so. And do refrain from calling her Jule, or girl. Her proper title is Lady. We expect you to use it."

Larry lowered his hand. "Hello . . . uh . . . Lady."

With her blue eyes, Lady swept each of them—Larry, Jane, and Strongheart—from head to feet. Then she sniffed and looked away.

"Hoity-toity," said Jane.

Strongheart rumbled in agreement.

Lady *was* hoity-toity. As cast and crew quickly learned, she was much too refined to slurp water from a communal dog bowl. She insisted on lapping from a delicate and handheld teacup.

She absolutely did *not* gulp down slabs of grilled beef brought in from the studio commissary. Rather, she nibbled marinated pigeon ordered from the finest French restaurants.

And she most certainly did *not* stretch out on the bare floor between takes. She reclined on soft cushions. A velvet pillow cradled her head.

Above all, Lady did *not* fraternize with police dogs. She was bossy and unfriendly and constantly found fault with Strongheart's behavior. Rushing at him, she nipped his backside for all sorts of petty reasons, like chewing on a toy she'd laid claim to, or wrestling with Pete between takes and disturbing her beauty rest, or squeaking his red rubber ball too loudly.

Only Larry's warning looks stopped Strongheart from nipping her back. Instead, he tucked in his tail and ran from her sharp white teeth . . . but not without tossing a few growls over his shoulder as he went.

The dogs' dislike for each other spilled over into their scenes.

"Cut!" shouted Larry toward the end of the first week of shooting. He lowered his megaphone and rubbed his forehead. "Listen, you two, this is supposed to be a romantic scene. We need sparks. Passion. Sizzle."

In response, Strongheart turned his back to the camera. He sat down regally on his bony haunches.

Lady *sniff-sniff*ed. Then she stuck her dainty muzzle in the air and stalked off the set.

"Did you say sizzle or fizzle?" drawled Jane.

Larry just groaned and covered his face with his hands.

During the second week of filming, cast and crew moved from the shooting stage to a nearby park. On their very first afternoon out, Lady approached Strongheart.

He got to his feet, ready to flee.

But Lady didn't rush at him. Instead, she flattened her ears ingratiatingly. Then she crouched, her rump in the air, her tail waving.

Strongheart just stood there.

She pounced and tugged on his ear.

Strongheart sat back on his haunches.

She gave an excited bark.

Strongheart blinked.

Then she somersaulted into him.

And memory flooded him: *he was wrestling with Otto, wriggling with Greta.*

Lady whined and ran a few steps into the underbrush. Then she stopped and looked back.

The tip of Strongheart's tail twitched. He took a tentative step toward her.

She scampered back and licked his face.
And Strongheart abandoned all his aloofness.

With a joyful, bounding leap, he ran—puppylike—
through meadow and wood, side by side with Lady.

Their newfound affection spilled over into their scenes.

Now they pulled the sled in perfect sync.

Their love scenes sizzled.

"Cut!" shouted Larry toward the end of their fourth week of shooting. He dropped his megaphone and applauded. "Yes! *That's* what I call acting."

Strongheart barked, then nuzzled his big head against Lady's.

She licked his nose.

"At least somebody's getting kissed around here," Jane muttered. Then, in a louder voice, she said, "There are times, Larry Trimble, when you really don't know onions about acting."

THE DOG KNOWS BEST

Strongheart stretched out in the shade of the jaca-randa tree. Filming was over. Until the movie opened in theaters, he had little to do but dawdle. His eyelids drooped. Every so often, he sighed happily.

Larry was stretched out, too. Flat on his back, his head resting on the dog's ribs, he dipped his hand into one of the many bags of fan mail the studio delivered each morning. Every so often, he read a letter aloud.

"I have seen *The Silent Call* twenty-three times and think you are the handsomest actor in Hollywood," gushed one fan.

"Do you wear a hairpiece on your tail to make it look so bushy?" asked another.

"Send me a picture of yourself," demanded still another. "And be sure to pawtograph it."

Strongheart opened one eye. *"Wurrrr!"*

"Bossy indeed," agreed Larry.

He fished out another letter. "Hey, listen to this one:"

Dear Mr. Strongheart,

We love you, We wish we could pet you. Please come visit us.

From your biggest fans, The kids at the Pacific Home for Orphaned Boys.

Strongheart opened both eyes. He scrambled to all fours. Barking sharply, he poked the letter with his snout.

"I knew you'd say that," said Larry.

The next afternoon, dog and director pulled up in front of the orphanage.

A circle of boys wearing threadbare hand-me-downs cheered as the famous shepherd bounded out of the car.

"Hiya, Strongheart!"

"Ain't he gorgeous?"

"Can we give him a treat, mister? We saved him some of our breakfast."

Sticky hands held out pieces of stale doughnuts and bits of cold bacon.

Strongheart trotted around the circle, accepting every bite. His muzzle brushed the boys' fingers like a soft kiss.

The boys grinned. They thumped the dog's sides and scratched behind his ears.

"I'm pettin' him!" cried one small boy. "I'm really pettin' him!"

Larry said, "Should we ask Strongheart to do some tricks?"

The boys cheered again.

And Strongheart ran through his repertoire: shake ... speak ... beg ... crawl ... roll over ... play dead.

"I'll need a volunteer for this next trick," said Larry.

The boys shrieked and bounced. Hands shot into the air.

Larry pointed to a tiny, gap-toothed kid wearing a pair of too-big knickers.

"What's your name?" he asked.

"Tommy," said the boy.

"Are you ready, Tommy?" asked Larry.

Tommy nodded. His face glowed with excitement.

And Larry turned to the dog. "Get the bad guy, Strongheart."

Strongheart ran at the boy. Growling playfully, he tugged at the length of rope holding up Tommy's too-big knickers.

Tommy squealed. Then giggled. Then squealed again.

"Okay, Strongheart, kiss and make up," said Larry.

SLURP!

The others hollered in delight.

Tommy flung his skinny arms around the dog's neck. "I love you, Strongheart!"

Strongheart gave him another slurp.

"Now, sadly, it's time for us to go," said Larry. "But we want to thank you boys for inviting us."

"Awww!" groaned the boys.

"Brrr-woof!" agreed Strongheart. He trailed after Larry toward the car. Suddenly, he stopped, one front paw off the ground. Turning his head, he stared at an older boy in the back row.

The boy jammed his fists into the pockets of his patched overalls. He took a nervous step backward—and knelt on the ground.

Strongheart lowered his head. His eyes never leaving the boy's, he stalked toward him.

The boy took another step backward.

Strongheart kept coming. He sniffed at the boy's front left pocket.

"Quit it!" hissed the boy. "Get lost."

Strongheart jumped up. Big paws pressed into bony shoulders.

"Get offa me, you galoot!" cried the boy.

Larry rushed over. "Strongheart, down!"

The dog did not obey.

"Down!" Larry shouted again.

Strongheart refused. He stared into the boy's face with unblinking eyes.

"Whaddya want from me?" The boy's lower lip trembled.

Strongheart hopped down, nosed the boy's front left pocket, then hopped back up.

The boy's hands were buried in the dog's fur now. Clutching. Clinging.

Strongheart's tongue dabbed his wet cheeks.

The boy rubbed his face against the dog's. At last, he sobbed, "I'm . . . I'm sorry."

With a last lick, Strongheart got down. He gave the boy a gentle nudge forward.

The boy sniffled. Hand trembling, he reached into his front pocket and pulled out a wallet. He gave it to Larry. "It's yours," he confessed. He lowered his head. "I pinched it while you was doing that trick with

Tommy. I shouldn't have. It was wrong."

"What's your name, son?"

Unable to meet Larry's eyes, the boy mumbled, "Frank Gowler, sir."

"Well, Frank, it's a wise man who listens to Strongheart. The dog knows best . . . or at least, he thinks he does."

"Hooray for Strongheart!" whooped Tommy.

"Hooray!" cheered the others.

Bouncing and swirling, Strongheart barked with delight. Then he hopped up on Frank again.

"Down," said Larry.

But Frank hugged the dog close. He laughed. "Naw, don't call him off, mister. I like it!"

They could see the Majestic Movie Palace from three blocks away. Its marquee blazed with lights, its blinking bulbs spelling out the words STRONGHEART IN *THE LOVE MASTER.*

In the backseat of the limousine, Mrs. Vanderbeek sniffed. "Lady Jule's name should be up there in lights, too. The poor darling has been positively ill since the studio chose not to include it."

Jane glanced over at the dogs. Snuggled together, they were taking turns squeaking Strongheart's red ball and licking each other's ears. Lady panted with an openmouthed grin.

"She looks like the berries to me," said Jane.

"I'm telling you," continued Mrs. Vanderbeek, "Lady's appetite has gone completely off. Would you believe she turned up her nose at the marinated pigeon from Le Chez? She wanted pickles and applesauce instead."

"Strongheart loves pickles," said Larry. "Especially with hamburgers."

Mrs. Vanderbeek ignored him. "And all the dear girl does is droop about the house, yawning and napping. I can't even interest her in a trip to the manicurist."

"Oh, that's applesauce," commiserated Jane.

"Pickles, too," added Mrs. Vanderbeek.

Larry shook his head. "Huh? You've lost me."

The limousine glided to the curb.

Beneath the theater's marquee, a crush of frenzied fans squealed. They pushed forward for a glimpse of the four-legged screen star.

Gossip reporter Lulu Popper leaned into her big silver microphone. "Hello from Hollywood! Tonight, dear listeners, I am broadcasting to you from the premiere of the year's most anticipated movie, *The Love Master,* starring that wonder dog of the silver screen, Strongheart. And here he comes now."

The limousine door opened. Strongheart and the others stepped out.

The crowd roared.

Pop! Flash! went the photographers' cameras.

"Doesn't he look marvelous?" reported Lulu. "Sleek and muscular, his coat a burnished black and tan. It appears he's left behind his red rubber ball. Rumor has it the star is wildly ... and secretly ... attached to the object. But tonight he is without his squeaker. Could it be that he has grown wildly attached to something— or *someone*—else?"

On the red carpet, Strongheart and Lady turned and posed.

Pop! Flash!

"And there's the movie's costar, Lady Jule. Isn't she a beauty? No wonder the king of dogdom has fallen head over paws in love. That's right, friends. You heard it *here* first. Sources tell me that during the making of this film, a *real* romance blossomed between the two."

Pop! Flash!

"Let's see if we can get an exclusive interview." Lulu waved a white-gloved hand. "Yoo-hoo, Mr. Strongheart! Mr. Strongheart! Won't you please answer a few questions for the millions of fans listening from coast to coast?"

Leaving his group behind on the red carpet, Strongheart trotted over to the gossip reporter. He held out his paw.

"Friends, you won't believe it," Lulu purred into the microphone. "I'm actually shaking hands with the prince of pooches. Believe me when I say I may never wash these fingers again."

Strongheart raised his muzzle. He sniffed the air.

"Let's not beat around the bush. Are the rumors true? Are you and Lady Jule in love?"

"Wurrrr!" he growled.

"Now, look, dear, I always ask personal questions. No need to get tetchy."

Strongheart whipped his head around and scanned the crowd. A savage look came into his eyes. His tail stiffened.

"Tell me. When do you and Lady Jule plan to tie the knot? I *must* be the first to know."

Strongheart's lips curled into a snarl, and the hair on his neck and shoulders rose. He crouched.

"You might as well spill it. Your fans—"

Strongheart's teeth flashed as he lunged into the crush of moviegoers, scattering them like startled sheep. His eyes locked on a curiously tall woman wobbling in her high-heeled shoes.

"Shoo!" she shouted in a deep, manly voice.

"Grrrrr," replied Strongheart. Leaping, he snatched the curly blond wig from her head to expose . . .

"Leroy 'Twitchy' Malone, the notorious bank robber!" squealed Lulu. "What a scoop!"

Twitchy turned and shoved his way through the crowd.

"My scoop is escaping!" cried Lulu.

Strongheart charged. Catching the bank robber by

an ankle, he knocked him flat. Then, grabbing one of his arms, he flipped Twitchy Malone over and stood on his chest, fangs bared and snarling.

Pop! Flash!

"Exclusive! Exclusive! In a sudden and thrilling turn of events, the police-dog-turned-screen-star has single-handedly—or should I say single-pawedly—captured one of the country's most notorious criminals. That's right, dear listeners. Strongheart—that wonder dog—is a true-life hero *off* the screen!"

She dragged her microphone over to Strongheart. "Do you have a few words for your admiring fans?"

"Brrr-woof!"

"And what about you, Mr. Malone? Any comments?"

Twitchy Malone groaned. "I wasn't planning to rob nothing. All's I wanted was to sneak out and see the new Strongheart picture. Who don't want to do that?"

"Who don't indeed," agreed Lulu. "Sadly, dear listeners, our time is over. I return you now to our studios and 'Musical Matinee.' And remember ... you heard it *here* first."

FOND FAREWELL

"Honestly, Jane, we'll hardly be gone any time at all," Larry said a few days later.

The two were standing in the driveway watching the taxicab driver load the suitcases—one for Larry and one for Strongheart.

Jane's eyes welled, and Larry handed her his handkerchief . . . again.

"I know. I know. It's just a two-week publicity tour," she said, and sniffled. "What's two weeks? The blink of the eye. A blip in time. So why can't I dry up?" She blew her nose loudly. "I feel like I'm saying goodbye to my own family."

"We *are* family," Larry replied.

Jane sucked in her breath. Her eyes shone.

"We're *Strongheart's* family," he concluded.

Jane exhaled, her breath sounding like a balloon deflating. "Well, don't look now, Big Daddy, but we're not the dog's only kin."

In the open doorway, Lady was all sighs, calf-eyes, and wiggling tail. Every so often, Strongheart turned and touched her neck with his muzzle.

"He has taken a shine to her," admitted Larry.

"A *shine*? You really don't know onions."

"What's that supposed to mean?"

"It's obvious—" began Jane.

The taxi driver honked.

"Got to go," interrupted Larry. He gave Jane's hand a brisk shake. "We'll call from New York." Climbing into the taxi, he whistled for the dog.

Strongheart gave Lady's ear one last lick. Then he grabbed his ball and hopped into the backseat, too.

Larry leaned out the car window. "Oh, and, Jane?"

"Yes?" She took a hopeful step toward him.

"Tell Mrs. Vanderbeek to go easy on the French food, will you? Lady is looking a bit . . . um . . . plump these days."

Jane covered the dog's ears. "Don't listen, Lady. He doesn't know what he's talking about."

The taxi drove away.

WHERE'S SOFIE?

At the train station in downtown Los Angeles, fans mobbed the movie star. So did the press.

"Look over here, Strongheart!"

Pop! Flash!

"Give us a noble pose!"

Pop! Flash!

"Now drop the ball and smile!"

Pop! Flash!

A girl stepped out of the crowd. A yellow hair bow almost the size of her freckled face stuck up from her bright red hair like a rooster's comb. Behind her stood a woman in a plumed hat and a short man with a bulbous nose.

"Go on now, Sofie," instructed the woman. "Give the nice doggie a kiss."

Sofie shook her head.

"Go ahead. Do it. Just like we said," urged the man.

Strongheart raised his muzzle and sniffed the air. A ridge of hair rose along his spine. He sniffed again.

That was when Sofie wrapped her thin arms around him.

Strongheart felt her heart fluttering against her bony chest like a panicked sparrow. He gave the girl's cheek a reassuring dab. She hugged him tighter. Then she bent and scooped up his ball.

"Brrr-woof!"

"Toss it to him," said Larry.

"You can do it," coaxed the woman.

The girl's face crumpled.

"Go on," said the man.

Sofie's eyes darted from the couple to the ball in her hand. Then she wound up and *heaved* it.

The ball bounced . . .

skittered . . .

ricocheted . . .

and rolled across the station's marble floor straight toward an open door marked

DANGER
UNDERGROUND TUNNELS
STAY OUT

For a moment, it wobbled on the edge of the top step. Then—*BUMP-BUMP-SQUEAK!*—it vanished into the gaping pitch-blackness.

Strongheart started after it.

"I'll get it!" cried Sofie. Yellow bow flopping, she dashed after the ball.

"Baby girl, come back!" called the woman.

"Stop!" shouted one of the reporters.

"Don't go down there!" cried Larry.

At the open door, Sofie paused for a second, squinting into the darkness. Then she squared her skinny shoulders and plunged down the stairs.

The woman screamed. "She's gone into the tunnel. Oh, my precious little Sofie! Somebody save her!"

Strongheart sprang into action. Plowing through the crowd, he hurtled across the station.

"No, Strongheart, wait!" Larry lurched forward.

Ignoring the command, Strongheart dove into the darkness, too.

Larry reached the doorway seconds later. "Bring a flashlight. Somebody bring a flashlight!"

The crowd pressed around him, gazing into the inky abyss. There was a hush. Then from below came the sound of muffled barking, followed by a high-pitched scream, a ferocious growl, and . . .

Silence.

"Sofie?" cried the woman.

A porter raced over with a flashlight. Larry fumbled with the switch. At last, a weak beam illuminated the dark entrance.

A beefy policeman pushed his way forward. "Stay back, people. Help is on the way."

"But my dog . . . ," began Larry.

"Our girl . . . ," said the man.

From below came a faint rustling.

"Sofie?"

A figure emerged from the gloom.

"Strongheart!"

His ears lay flat. His tail drooped. And in his mouth he carried a yellow bow. From it trailed a single strand of bright red hair.

IT'S THE LULU POPPER RADIO HOUR

Lulu Popper leaned into her big silver microphone. "Hello from Hollywood. Today, dear listeners, I'm broadcasting to you from the sidewalk of the Los Angeles County jail. That's right, friends, *jail*. And do I have a hot wire for you. That king of dogdom, box-office darling, and idol to millions, Strongheart, has been tossed into a cell and locked behind bars. Yes, dear listeners. He's been *arrested*!"

Lulu paused dramatically to let the news sink in. "The alleged victim is six-year-old Sofie Bedard, who mysteriously disappeared yesterday afternoon from the tunnels beneath Central Station. Police have scoured the area to no avail. Not a trace of the girl remains. Is it foul play? Could the four-legged actor be involved? We'll have more after this word from our sponsor."

As an announcer broke in with the commercial, Lulu gestured to the couple from the train station, who had been standing to the side. "Don't be nervous. Just relax and be yourselves," she advised.

"We ain't nervous," huffed the woman. "We want that Strongheart to pay for what he done."

"And pay *big*," added the man.

The woman nodded, the feather trim of her hat bouncing in crisp agreement. "Once folks hear what we got to say . . . well . . . it's downright shocking."

"Shocking," echoed the man.

Lulu's eyebrows rose almost to her hairline. But there was no time to ask questions . . . at least off-air.

She leaned into her microphone again. "Welcome back, dear listeners. We are here with Fred and Mildred Bedard, the parents of little Sofie—"

Mr. Bedard interrupted her. "Now, see, we ain't exactly the girl's—"

Mrs. Bedard stopped him with a jab of her elbow. "Let. Lulu. Talk." She cast him a knowing look.

Mr. Bedard caught it. "Oh . . . um . . . sure. Go on ahead, Lulu."

"Yes, well," said Lulu. She cleared her throat. "Let's get right to it. Tell me, Fred and Mildred, what do you think really happened to your little girl?"

Mr. Bedard grabbed the microphone. "It was that . . . that *fiend,* that dog, Strongheart." He spat out the last word as if it tasted bad. "He went down into the basement after our baby girl. Everyone thought he was rescuing her, but now . . . now . . ."

Mrs. Bedard snatched up the story. "We heard her

screaming. And Strongheart snarling. Our Sofie, she was a bitsy thing, not much bigger than a jackrabbit. It would have been easy."

"Are you suggesting . . . ," began Lulu.

Mr. Bedard interrupted. "A girl and a dog went in. But the only *living* thing that came out was the dog."

"Oh my," said Lulu.

"Go on, Fred," urged Mrs. Bedard. "Tell them the rest. Tell them what he done."

Mr. Bedard sputtered. "He . . . he *et* her, that's what! Clothes and all. That's how come she vanished without a trace. He *et* her."

"That's right," chimed in Mrs. Bedard. "Strongheart et our Sofie-girl all up!"

STRONGHEART, SAD AND SCARED

The gates of the police kennel slammed shut behind Strongheart.

Memories rushed at him: *Sharp boot kicks. Angry voices. Drilling, marching, and snapping to commands.*

With a low, half-sobbing whine, Strongheart *sniff-sniff*ed along the bottom of the heavy door for a whiff of comfort.

Nothing.

His ears keyed for the sound of a familiar step.

Still nothing.

In the middle of the concrete floor, he sat and pointed his nose at the ceiling.

"Aaaaaarrrooooo!"

His howls were full-throated and sorrowful, surging upward in heartbreaking waves, dying down into trembling sobs, then surging upward again with rush after rush of grief.

They went on for a long time.

After that, he lay on the floor, his eyes dull, his head drooping. Food didn't interest him. Neither did the twice-daily walk around the exercise yard. The world had once again become a bleak place without warmth, a place where caresses and kind words did not exist.

At night, in the cold loneliness of his cell, Strongheart dreamed . . . about the warm weight of Larry's head on his ribs and the cheerful *clickety-clack-ding* of Jane's typewriter; about the *SQUEAK-SQUEAK* of his red rubber ball, and the smell of marinated pigeon on Lady's soft breath.

And in his sleep, Strongheart sighed.

REUNION

Days later, a voice boomed, "You've got a visitor."

Strongheart dragged himself to his feet. He looked toward the door.

It opened. There stood Larry.

"Ten minutes," boomed the voice.

Larry strode halfway across the cell. "Strongheart, oh, Strongheart! Did you think I'd abandoned you, buddy? They wouldn't let me visit until today. But I'm here now." He squatted and opened his arms.

Strongheart did not rush forward. Instead, he watched and waited. The tip of his tail quivered.

"Come on, pal. Give me a hug!"

Strongheart went to him. Not with a leap, but quickly and eagerly. Thrusting his head forward, he burrowed in between Larry's arm and body. He pressed close to his best friend.

The two snuggled for several long minutes.

Then Strongheart pulled away. He trotted expectantly toward the door.

Larry shook his head. "I'm sorry, boy, but I can't take you home. Not yet." He explained about the charges against Strongheart. "The trial has been set for next week."

Strongheart trembled.

"Try not to worry. I've hired a top-notch lawyer, the best in the state. Virgil Gance. He's never lost a case."

Strongheart sagged onto his blanket. His big head drooped.

"Two minutes!" boomed the voice.

"I know it looks bad now, buddy, but you must keep your chin up. Once the judge hears the whole story, he'll have to find you innocent. He'll just *have* to."

Strongheart closed his eyes.

"Until then, I'll visit every day. I promise."

"Time's up," boomed the voice.

"Not yet," begged Larry. He dug into his pocket. "Look, Strongheart, I brought you a new ball. A green one this time. Nice, isn't it?" He gave the toy an inviting squeak. "Catch it, boy. Come on!" He tossed it to the dog.

But Strongheart just turned his head.

The ball rolled into a corner.

It sat there . . . unsqueaked.

TRIAL AND TRIBULATIONS

Spectators packed the courtroom. Whispering, necks craning, they looked toward where Strongheart sat—along with Larry and Virgil Gance—at the counsel table. Fans tried to sneak to the front, and the bailiff shooed them away like flies. "And that goes for you, too," he bellowed at the reporters.

Strongheart paid no attention to any of it. Poised and tense, he stared straight ahead. He turned only when Jane called from the spectator area, "Lady sends her love. She also has news. She's . . ."

The bailiff called out, "All rise. Court will convene in the case of the State of California versus Strongheart. The honorable Judge Bertram Seitz presiding."

Judge Seitz swept up to the bench. Once seated, he turned to the prosecutor. "You may call your first witness."

The prosecutor nodded. "Will Artie Figgins take the witness stand, please?"

"Who?" whispered Larry.

A pudgy, balding man rose from the crowd.

"Hey, that's the pickpocket!" hissed Larry.

Figgins took the witness stand.

"Mr. Figgins," began the prosecutor, "you were employed as a studio hand on the set of Strongheart's first movie, *The Silent Call*. Is that correct?"

"That's right," said the witness.

"And while you were on this job, did you ever see Mr. Strongheart behave ferociously?"

"I didn't see it. I *experienced* it. He attacked me . . . out of the clear blue!"

"Would you tell us about that?"

Figgins looked toward the jury. "I was running the arc light for Strongheart's first scene. He was standing all dramatic-like on a cliff, the camera grinding away, when all of a sudden he turned. And he looked at me." Figgins shivered. "His icy gaze . . . I'll never forget it.

There was murder in his eyes. Cold-blooded murder."

The courtroom buzzed.

"What happened next?"

"He charged me, knocked me to the ground, and pressed his razor-sharp teeth to my jugular. I'm telling you, a few more seconds and he'd have ripped my throat out."

"Thank you, Mr. Figgins. One final question. In your opinion, is Strongheart capable of consuming a child?"

"Capable?" replied the witness. "Why, I'd be surprised if he hasn't eaten a *dozen* kids already."

Spectators gasped.

Reporters scribbled furiously.

And Larry leaped up. "Objection!"

"You can't object, Mr. Trimble," said the judge. "You are not a lawyer."

"But that man's a thief!" cried Larry. "He was stealing on the set. He's holding a grudge because Strong-heart caught him red-handed. None of it happened the way he said."

Judge Seitz hammered his gavel. "Sit down or I'll have you removed from my courtroom."

"But . . . he . . ."

Strongheart gave Larry's sleeve a tug.

Still sputtering, the director sat.

Now the prosecutor began calling a string of surprising witnesses.

Ed Brady took the stand. "Yeah, sure, I was knocked around by Strongheart on the set. . . . That's right, he did shred my costume with his teeth. . . . Was I scared at the time? Terrified, but he was just *acting* vicious. The dog's a great actor, for Pete's sake. . . . How do I know he's not really a fierce dog pretending to be nice?" Ed shrugged. "You got me there. I guess I don't."

At the counsel table, Strongheart hung his head.

The schnauzer-owning woman from the ship's gangplank testified next. Her three chins trembled as she said, "I do not exaggerate when I say that I snatched my sweet pookie-kins from the very jaws of death. That beast was *this close* to gobbling her up."

Strongheart hung his head a bit lower.

"I call Sergeant Friedrich Brotz of the Berlin Police Department to the stand," said the prosecutor.

Spectators leaned forward in their seats as the uniformed officer with the booming voice told of the dog's early life. "Etzel? He was the fiercest, most aggressive police dog in our kennel. We trained him to be merciless. . . . You ask if such a dog can be rehabilitated? *Nein*. Once a killer, always a killer."

The courtroom buzzed again.

And Strongheart's head hung so low his chin rested on the table.

STRONGHEART TAKES THE STAND

"Do you wish to call any further witnesses?" Judge Seitz asked the prosecutor.

"No, Your Honor," the prosecutor replied. "I think we've made our case."

"Then we shall proceed with the defense." The judge turned toward the counsel table. "Mr. Gance."

The lawyer stood. "Your Honor, I wish to call Strongheart to the stand."

"Objection!" shouted the prosecutor. "This is preposterous, Your Honor. How can the dog give testimony? He can't talk."

"But he *can* communicate," replied Gance.

"How?" retorted the prosecutor.

"In the same way he communicates with millions of moviegoers each and every day," replied Gance. "Through expression and gesture."

The judge pondered for several moments. "I'll allow it," he finally said.

"Your Honor . . . ," began the prosecutor.

The judge cut him off with a sharp rap of the gavel.

A hushed babble of excitement rose from the courtroom as Strongheart came forward. He hesitated before taking his place in front of the judge's bench. Looking out across the courtroom, he trembled and a soft whine escaped his lips.

This was THE BIG SCENE.

Gance approached. "Would you tell us—in your own actions—what happened that morning in the train tunnels?"

Strongheart did not respond. He sat stone still. Not a muscle twitched.

At the counsel table, Larry squeezed his hands together. "Come on, boy," he muttered. "You can do this."

Strongheart looked down at the floor, like he was trying to remember.

The courtroom held its breath and waited.

At last, he stood. Sweeping his nose back and forth in a wide arc, he sniffed along the courtroom floor.

"So you searched for the girl by following her scent," interpreted Gance. "Did you find her?"

Strongheart wagged his tail wildly. He yipped with joy.

"I will take that to mean 'yes,'" said the judge. "But if you found the child, why isn't she with us today? What happened?"

Strongheart's demeanor changed. His eyes took on a savage look, and his lips curled back, exposing sharp teeth. He crouched, ready to spring, as a deep-throated growl rumbled up from his throat.

A shocked gasp ran through the courtroom.

"The dog has just proven my case," declared the prosecutor. "Look at him. A killer!"

"Your Honor," argued Gance. "The dog is simply reenacting his behavior in the tunnels that day. Obviously, he encountered some sort of threat or danger down there. Is that correct, Strongheart?"

"Wurrr-woof! Wurrr-woof! Wurrr-woof!"

"Objection!" cried the prosecutor again. "He's putting words in the dog's mouth."

"Overruled," snapped the judge. Leaning over the bench, he asked, "What happened next, Strongheart?"

The dog mimicked desperation. Rushing forward, he leaped, circled, sniffed, whirled.

"Are you telling this court you believe someone else was down in the tunnels that day?" asked Gance. "And this person took Sofie?"

Strongheart wagged his tail "yes."

"That dog's a liar!" shouted Mrs. Bedard, rising from the crowd.

"A low-down, doggone liar," chimed in Mr. Bedard.

Larry sprang out of his chair. "You take that back!"

"Give it to 'em, Larry!" hollered Jane. She boxed at the air.

Judge Seitz banged his gavel. "Silence!"

"They can't badmouth my dog like that. Why, I ought to—"

"Sit!"

Red-faced and breathing hard, Larry grudgingly obeyed. So did the others, but not before Jane poked out her tongue at Mildred Bedard.

The judge pretended not to see. Instead, he returned to Strongheart. "What happened after you lost the girl?"

Strongheart demonstrated. Once again, he sniffed along the floor, pantomiming his search for clues. At the evidence table, he stopped. Only one item sat on it—Sofie's big yellow hair ribbon. Strongheart took it in his mouth just as he had when he'd found it lying on the tunnel floor. With heavy steps, he carried it back to the bench and laid it at the judge's feet. His ears lay flat. His tail sagged. His eyes were downcast, as if there was a weight in his soul.

"A powerful performance," drawled the prosecutor. "But it still doesn't answer the most important question: What happened to little Sofie Bedard?"

His words chilled the courtroom into silence.

"Any further witnesses, Mr. Gance?" asked the judge.

"No, Your Honor."

"Then we will adjourn until tomorrow morning."

ORPHANS TO THE RESCUE

In the upper dormitory of the Pacific Home for Orphaned Boys, Frank Gowler heaved a shoe at the radio.

"Aw, shut up you gobstoppin' old buttinsky!"

The shoe missed.

Lulu Popper's nasally twang filled the room. "Things are looking bad for that wonder dog, Strongheart. Is he a cold-blooded murderer or a harmless actor? That's the million-dollar question. And *this* reporter has the answer. Reliable sources tell me that despite the star's brilliant courtroom performance, the jury will pronounce him a danger and the judge will lock him away forever. His Hollywood-made fortune, meanwhile, will be given to the unfortunate Bedards. No, dear listeners, money cannot replace a child. But perhaps it will provide some small measure of comfort in their hour of—"

THUMP!

The second shoe hit its mark. The room filled with static.

"Why'd you do that?" grumbled one of the boys.

"I'm sick and tired of that biddy's flapping tongue," fumed Frank. "Strongheart ain't vicious. He ain't no kid killer. He's a good dog. The *best* dog."

"Sure he is," agreed Tommy.

"So what are we gonna do about it?" asked Frank. "Just sit around while they toss him in the clink and throw away the key?"

"What else *can* we do?" asked one of the boys. "We can't just leave. We'll get in trouble."

"What's a little trouble to help out Strongheart?" replied Frank. "Didn't he put me on the path to the straight and narrow? Didn't he make little Tommy here laugh? Gosh, fellas, didn't he bring us all a little happiness?"

Heads around the room nodded.

"Whaddya say? Are you with me?"

"I am!" cried Tommy, tugging up his too-big knickers.

"Me too," said another boy.

"And me," said another.

"So what are we are waiting for?" said Frank. "Let's spread out, ask questions, knock on doors if we have to." He walked to the window and lifted the sash. "It's out there, fellas—I just know it—some little clue that'll prove Strongheart's innocence. Even if it takes all night, we gotta find it."

One by one, the boys swung their legs over the sill and climbed down the magnolia tree that hugged the side of the building.

They sprinted into the night.

LARRY, SAD AND SCARED

Larry sat on the sofa, clutching Strongheart's pillow to his chest. "How will he be able to endure that cold, hard place without us . . . without his family?" He sniffled and turned to Jane. "And how can I go on without him . . . without my best friend?"

A knot of love and worry wedged in Jane's throat. Moving across the room, she knelt in front of him and put her hands over his. "No, Larry, you can't think that way. You have to stay positive."

Larry blinked back tears. "You were there, Jane. You saw how still the courtroom got. It reminded me of the eerie calm that comes right before a bad storm." He swallowed hard. "After tomorrow's whirlwind, my life—and his—will be nothing but ruins."

"Ruins?" Jane said, her eyes welling. "Even if Strongheart *is* found guilty, we'll still have each other. And that . . . that's *something*."

Larry nodded. Leaning forward, he wiped a tear from her cheek.

Jane raised her quivering chin. "We have to stick together. We have to keep fighting for Strongheart's freedom even if it means taking on every cockeyed judge in this state. And we won't stop until he's home."

Just then a tiny whimper floated through the open bedroom doorway.

"Home with *all* of us," Jane managed to add.

Larry blinked. "All of us," he repeated.

Wrapping their arms around each other, they cried.

GUILTY OR INNOCENT?

The bailiff led Strongheart into the courtroom and over to the counsel table.

"Good luck to you, Mr. Strongheart," he said as he unclipped the dog's leash. "I'm a big fan. I sure hope after today you'll be free to make more movies."

Strongheart gave the man's hand a quick dab of thanks. Then he hopped up into the seat between Larry and Mr. Gance. He panted heavily.

Larry reached over and rubbed the dog's neck. Beneath Strongheart's thick fur, his muscles felt tense and knotted. "Easy, boy," Larry soothed.

Strongheart panted harder.

Spectators began scurrying into the courtroom. "The jury has reached a verdict!" someone exclaimed. "The judge is coming in now."

Across the aisle, the prosecutor smiled smugly.

"He seems confident," Larry said to Gance.

The lawyer nodded. "Sometimes you get a sixth sense about what the jury is thinking."

"And what *is* the jury thinking?"

Looking grim, Gance shook his head.

Larry sagged.

"Hear ye, hear ye," shouted the bailiff. "Court will reconvene in the case of the state versus Strongheart."

Taking a seat at the bench, Judge Seitz silently read the jury's decision. Then he cleared his throat and looked at the dog.

A nervous hush filled the courtroom.

"This has been a difficult case," began the judge. "Yes, Strongheart is a handsome, talented actor. But he has also been shown to be a vicious dog, capable of . . ."

The courtroom doors burst open.

"Stop the trial!" shouted Frank.

He charged up the aisle, followed by a gang of blurry-eyed, smudge-faced boys.

"What's going on here?" bellowed the judge.

"Strongheart's innocent. We got proof!" cried Tommy.

"Let me do the talking, will you?" Frank stepped forward. "It's like this, Mr. Judge, sir. Me and the boys here, we found some evidence we think you should see."

"What kind of evidence?"

"Show him, fellas."

The circle of boys opened to reveal . . .

"Sofie?" gasped Mr. Bedard.

A murmur of surprise ran through the courtroom.

And Strongheart gave a joyful yip.

Mrs. Bedard blinked twice. "Yer . . . yer . . . alive! Look, Fred, Sofie's alive. And she's standing right here. *In court.*"

Mr. Bedard ran both his hands through his hair. "I'm seeing it, but I ain't believing it."

The judge leaned forward. "Are *you* Sofie Bedard?"

She shook her head. "No, sir."

A hush fell over the courtroom.

"Then who are you?" the judge asked.

"I'm Sofie Parker. Bedard is my aunt and uncle's last name." She pointed to the couple. "That's them over there. I'm visiting for the summer. From Ohio."

"I see."

Mrs. Bedard waved her arm. "Yer Honor, the girl obviously ain't right in her head. She's talking gibberish."

"Most likely from that vicious attack," added Mr. Bedard.

"That's not true." Sofie blinked, her eyes suddenly wet. "We lied . . . to get his money."

A shocked murmur ran through the courtroom.

"Go on, Sofie," said the judge.

"I . . . I'm so sorry. So sorry." She cried harder.

Frank dropped to one knee and looked her in the face. "I know how you feel. But don'tcha see? The truth is the only way to make things right." He nodded to Strongheart. "A smart dog taught me that."

Sofie hiccupped and wiped her eyes on her sleeve. "It . . . it all started when we were listening to the report of the premiere of *The Love Master* on the radio," she said to the judge. "Lulu Popper was saying how Strongheart almost never went anywhere without his ball. And that gave Aunt Mildred an idea."

"What happened next?" asked the judge.

"Aunt Mildred said it'd be easy as apple pie. She knew from the newspaper that Strongheart was going to be at the train station for the start of his publicity tour. "'Get ahold of the dog's ball,' she told me. 'Throw it into the train tunnel and run down after it.'"

"How did she know the dog would go after you?"

Sofie shrugged as if stating the obvious. "Strongheart is a hero."

Her words were met with claps and whistles.

Judge Seitz banged his gavel.

Sofie took a deep breath and went on. "Uncle Fred planned the rest. He got his friend, Mr. Kelley, to unlock the door. Mr. Kelley works at the train station, and he knows all its secret ins and outs. That's who fetched me from the tunnel." She shuddered. "He sure took his time about it, though. I was scared in the dark. I even screamed once."

"And then?"

"I pulled out my hair ribbon and dropped it on the ground like I'd been told. Mr. Kelley took me to stay with his family. He's got seven kids, so who'd notice one more? I've been hiding out with them ever since."

"Until *we* found you!" exclaimed Tommy.

The judge looked from one to the other. "And just how did you do that?"

"We followed the Bedards," one of the boys replied.

"Just like them private detectives in dime novels do," piped up Tommy.

The courtroom burst into laughter.

Frank picked up the story. "At first they didn't go anywhere interesting. A diner. The park. But finally, early this morning, Mr. Bedard stopped in at a boardinghouse over on Pico Street. We could hear kids inside, so Tommy here—"

"Let me tell this part, Frank." Tommy puffed up his scrawny chest. "I shinnied up the drainpipe and peeked in a window and there she was—Sofie—sitting on the bed and sobbing her eyes out. I knew it was her from all the newspaper pictures."

"We talked her into coming with us," added another boy.

"And saved Strongheart!" declared Tommy.

Frank stepped closer to the bench. "We *have* saved him, haven't we, Mr. Judge, sir?"

"You sure have, son." The judge banged his gavel. "This case is dismissed. Strongheart, you are free to go."

The courtroom erupted into cheers and whistles.

Larry flung his arms around the dog and gave him a big kiss on the nose.

Strongheart lick . . . lick . . . licked him back. Then he raised his head and barked with everything he could put into it.

With sheer joy and in a single bound, he leaped over the counsel table. Barreling headfirst into Frank, he slopped his tongue all over the boy's face.

"Knock it off, Strongheart," laughed Frank, even as he wrapped his arms around the dog and rolled with him on the floor.

The other boys rushed them. Petting. Rubbing. Thumping. Hugging.

Strongheart barked again and again.

In the ruckus, no one noticed the Bedards being led away in handcuffs.

But Strongheart did notice the little girl standing teary-eyed by the bench. Padding over to her, he nudged her hand.

Shyly, she curled her fingers into his thick fur.

He nuzzled her cheek, and she reached into her pocket and pulled out a red rubber ball. "I kept it for you," she said. She held it out.

Strongheart looked at it a moment. Then he picked it up in his mouth, gave it a tender squeak, and put it back in her still-outstretched hand.

"For me?" She smiled. "Thank you."

Around them, the boys were still cheering, spectators were still clapping, and Jane was still whooping, "We won! He's coming home! We—"

She was silenced by a big *SMOOOOOCH*!

Reeling, she gripped the back of a chair for support. "What in the world?"

"Jane Murfin," cried Larry, "you are the bee's knees!"

She wrapped her arms around his neck. "It's about time you got on the trolley." She kissed him back.

SURPRISE

On the courthouse steps, fans mobbed the movie star.

Reporters peppered him with questions.

Cameras *pop-flash*ed.

Lulu Popper begged for an exclusive.

But Strongheart rushed past them. It was obvious to all that he wanted just one thing: he wanted to go home.

At the bungalow, he jumped from the backseat before the taxi finished braking. He raced for the door.

Larry and Jane ran after him.

Turning the knob with his teeth, he pushed into the house. He barked wildly for Lady.

Jane put her finger to her lips. "Shhhh! You'll wake the . . ."

A chorus of whimpers and squeals rose into the air.

"Too late," said Larry.

Strongheart cocked his ears. Cautious now, he followed the sound until he reached the darkened bedroom. There lay Lady. Three pudgy puppies nestled in the curve of her warm belly.

Strongheart looked up at Larry.

"Incredible, huh?" said Larry. "It was a complete surprise."

"Not for *some* of us," Jane corrected him.

Strongheart moved forward. Gently, he lowered himself to the floor.

Lady wagged and lightly licked him on the neck. Then she nudged one of the puppies toward him.

The infant sprawled in front of Strongheart. The big dog watched with curiosity as the pup squeaked and wiggled. Then he extended his head and sniffed the baby. Their noses met, and a tiny warm tongue touched Strongheart's muzzle.

The other puppies wobbled forward. They tripped and tumbled over him. They nipped his ears. They yipped with milky-sweet breath. And the sudden memory of a sun-washed farmyard came to him: *three puppies chasing and splashing and snuggling together.*

Strongheart looked around with wondering eyes. At Larry and Jane. At Lady and their puppies.

A family.

The big dog sighed.

His family.

THE TRUTH BEHIND THIS TALE

While this story is fiction, it is based on true events. Back in the 1920s, there really was a movie-star dog named Strongheart. And he was indeed owned by director Larry Trimble and screenwriter Jane Murfin. Hitting upon the idea of developing a dramatic dog actor, Larry and Jane traveled around the United States looking for the perfect canine. In one version of events, they found him at a kennel in White Plains, New York. But in another version, unable to discover the ideal dog in America, they searched across Europe. Not until they arrived in Berlin did they find him—a fierce, highly trained three-year-old German shepherd police dog named Etzel von Oeringen. Larry recalled their first meeting: "We had gotten about twenty feet inside the fence when there came a sudden crash of glass and a horrible growl and [the dog] came through a front window . . . and was tearing across the lawn at us—a fearsome sight indeed."

Larry saw past Etzel's fierceness to his star potential. Taking him back to Hollywood, the couple renamed him Strongheart and began planning his movie career. While Jane wrote a screenplay, Larry worked at teaching him how to play. It wasn't easy. The dog, recalled Larry, "had never played with a child, had never known the fun of retrieving a ball or stick; had never been petted; in short, had never been a dog." Using a squeaky rubber ball, Larry taught Strongheart to fetch, catch, and play tag. Soon the ball became the dog's favorite, and constant, toy.

Strongheart's first movie, *The Silent Call,* was released in 1921. It was a blockbuster. Not only did it gross one million dollars (an astronomical amount in those days), but movie critics swooned over Strongheart's acting ability. *Photoplay* magazine called him "dramatic . . . emotional . . . one of the most intelligent dogs that ever lived." And the *New York Times* wrote, "[He] is not one of your tiresome trick dogs, but an independent actor."

Magazines soon clamored for the chance to photograph him. Reporters begged to write feature stories about him. And fans inundated him with cards and letters. As many as five bags of fan mail a day arrived at the studio. Americans were so taken with the dog that within one year of the film's release, German shepherds became the most popular dog breed in the country. A brand of dog food was even named after him. Strongheart Dog Food is still made today.

The star became more popular still when he met his mate, Lady Jule (Lady Julie, by some accounts), while filming *The Love Master.* According to the *New York Times,* Strongheart "picked his leading lady from forty other dogs . . . and the real romance of these canines developed." Reporters quickly took to calling the dogs "Mr. and Mrs. Strongheart" and joyfully reported the birth in December 1923 of "six little sons and daughters to bless the Strongheart home."

Two months after the puppies' arrival, the couple set out on a cross-country publicity tour. Traveling by train in a luxurious private compartment, they stopped in towns and cities along the route. At every station, crowds gathered and brass bands played. Time and again, Strongheart solemnly stood as a mayor hung the key to his city around the dog's neck.

In New York City, the couple presided over the Westminster Dog Show, where they sat on a high dais pressing their "pawtographs" onto glossy black-and-white photos for their fans. Strongheart also tangled with an English terrier named Lord Algernon who came sniffing around Lady Jule. According to one reporter, Strongheart grabbed Lord Algernon by his well-groomed neck and "shook the intruder to a frazzle, sending him back to his kennel a sadder, but wiser dog."

It wasn't the only time Strongheart exhibited his police-dog aggressiveness. He was forever sniffing out people with bad intentions. Claimed Larry, "He often pursued passersby later found to have been embezzlers [or] frauds." On one occasion, Strongheart chased an imposter reporter out of Larry's backyard. On another, he pounced on a thieving banker.

Unfortunately, this habit landed him in trouble. In August 1928, the family of six-year-old Sofie Bedard accused Strongheart of attacking the girl. He tried, they claimed, to eat her. Hollywood buzzed over the allegations. But the case never went to trial. That's because lawyers quickly uncovered the truth—the Bedards were lying in hopes of extorting money from Larry and Jane. All charges against the movie-star dog were dropped. The Bedards, however, were brought before a judge for lying to the court.

Strongheart made a total of six films, all of them box-office hits. But his career was cut short in early 1929 when he fell against a hot lamp while on a movie set and severely burned his leg. Veterinarians did all they could, but Strongheart did not recover. He died that June at the age of thirteen. Newspapers across the country marked his passing. "He was a king of dogdom," declared the *Joplin Globe* in Missouri. "Wise, virile, afire with energy . . . may he have a happy role to play in dog heaven."

Sadly, only Strongheart's last film, *The Return of Boston Blackie,* can still be seen today. Watching it, one can understand why moviegoers fell in love with the dog. Strongheart is big and handsome, his expression is alert, and his movements are quick and graceful. No wonder fans nicknamed him the Wonder Dog.

You can see Strongheart's acting abilities for yourself online: youtube.com/watch?v=IN1VyUhnDyI.

And check out this newsreel of Strongheart and Lady Jule taken at the McAlpin Hotel in New York City during their cross-country publicity tour: youtube .com/watch?v=gWZlpRqIVJ4.

Strongheart's Movies
The Silent Call (1921)
Brawn of the North (1922)
The Love Master (1924)
North Star (1925)
White Fang (1925)
The Return of Boston Blackie (1927)

THE REAL STRONGHEART

Strongheart shows off his star power in this publicity shot taken for *The Silent Call* in 1921.

Jane Murfin and Strongheart in their Beverly Hills backyard in 1922.

A publicity photo of Strongheart and Lady Jule taken on the set of
The Love Master in 1924. Note the dogs' pawtographs at the bottom.

An alert Strongheart shares a boulder with best friend and
director Larry Trimble around 1924.

BIBLIOGRAPHY

Boone, J. Allen. *Kinship with All Life.* New York: HarperOne, 1976.

"Dog Star Red Cross Vet," *Los Angeles Times,* August 2, 1925, latimesblogs.latimes.com.

"Here and Abroad," *The New York Times,* September 9, 1923, timesmachine.nytimes.com.

Howe, Herbert. "Close-Ups and Long Shots," *Photoplay,* January 1924, archive.org.

Klumph, Helen. "Strongheart Pulls Some Star Stuff," *Picture Play,* June 1924, archive.org.

Murfin, Jane. "Writing for a Dog Star," *The New York Times,* June 17, 1923, timesmachine.nytimes.com.

Orlean, Susan. *Rin Tin Tin.* New York: Simon & Schuster, 2011.

"Picture Plays and People," *The New York Times,* February 13, 1924, timesmachine.nytimes.com.

"The Screen." *The New York Times,* January 30, 1922, timesmachine.nytimes.com.

"Strongheart Is No More," *Joplin (Missouri) Globe,* June 26, 1929, newspaperarchive.com.

"Strongheart, Movie Dog Star, Proves Attraction at Show," *The New York Times,* February 13, 1924, timesmachine.nytimes.com.

"Strongheart Visits the *Times.*" *The New York Times,* February 17, 1924, timesmachine.nytimes.com.

"Throngs Pay Honor to Dogdom's Elite," *The New York Times,* February 13, 1922, timesmachine.nytimes.com.

Trimble, Lawrence. *Strongheart: The Story of a Wonder Dog.* Racine, Wisconsin: Whitman Publishing Company, 1926.

Trimble, Lawrence. "The Story of Strongheart," *Photoplay,* December 1921: 48, 96.

Trimble, Lawrence. "Teaching a Dog to Act," *The New York Times,* May 18, 1924, timesmachine.nytimes.com.

York, Cal. "Studio News and Gossip," *Photoplay,* May 1924, archive.org.

NOTES

"We had gotten . . .": Trimble, *Strongheart: The Story of a Wonder Dog,* np.

"had never played . . .": Trimble, "The Story of Strongheart," 48.

"dramatic . . . emotional . . . one . . .": Orlean, 60.

"[He] is not one . . .": *The New York Times,* January 30, 1922, 18.

"picked his leading lady . . .": *The New York Times,* February 13, 1924, 14.

"Mr. and Mrs. Strongheart": Klumpf, 22.

"six little sons . . .": Howe, 51.

"pawtographs": Klumpf, 22.

"shook the intruder . . .": York, 95.

"He often pursued . . .": Trimble, "The Story of Strongheart," 49.

"He was a king . . .": *Joplin Globe,* June 26, 1929, 3.

ABOUT THE AUTHOR AND ILLUSTRATOR

CANDACE FLEMING is the author of numerous award-winning books for young people, including the nonfiction titles *The Family Romanov,* winner of the *Boston Globe–Horn Book Award,* the NCTE Orbis Pictus Award, and a Robert F. Sibert Honor; *Amelia Lost,* a *New York Times* Notable Children's Book; and *The Great and Only Barnum,* an ALA-YALSA Best Book for Young Adults. She is also the author of the hilarious novels *Ben Franklin's in My Bathroom!* and *The Fabled Fourth Graders of Aesop Elementary,* among others.

ERIC ROHMANN received the Caldecott Medal for *My Friend Rabbit* and the Caldecott Honor for *Time Flies.* He is also the author and illustrator of the highly acclaimed *A Kitten Tale* and *Bone Dog.*

This is Candace and Eric's fourth collaboration. Their previous titles include *Oh, No!; Bulldozer's Big Day;* and, most recently, *Giant Squid,* a Robert F. Sibert Honor Book. They both live in Chicago. Visit them online at candacefleming.com and ericrohmann.com